DARK WITCH

PREQUEL TO THE FRONTIER WITCHES SERIES

ANNETTE GRANTHAM

"One for sorrow,

two for mirth,

three for a funeral,

and four for a birth."

CHAPTER ONE

IN THE BLOSSOMING DAYS of spring in 1820, Bridget Gilhooley and her sister, Ellen, received an urgent message from their elder sister, Margaret. Their young niece, Lillian, was in trouble. Concerned, they made their way to Margaret's cottage on the outskirts of Manorhamilton, Ireland, fearing the worst.

But, as they approached, their anxiety dissolved into peals of laughter. The garden before them erupted with vibrant colors and intoxicating scents, as if summer had arrived early. Foxgloves, lavender, and comfrey spilled over the flower beds, while furze blossoms adorned the stone fence, enveloping the air with a sweet coconut fragrance.

Bridget remarked, "Our little niece, Lillian, is an earth witch. Quite an early manifestation. Our irritable sister won't be pleased." The garden was a welcome addition to the house, providing a lush backdrop that softened its shabby appearance.

Margaret, her face flushed and her legs entangled by winding cucumber vines, shouted, "Bas!" as she pointed at the plants, causing them to wilt back into the ground.

Ellen furrowed her brows. "Looks like Margaret is furious. She's going to tucker herself out. There are too many plants to curse."

Bridget pushed open the gate, traversing a thick carpet of red clover. "Isn't she always? She's putting on a show now that we're here."

Margaret's face contorted into a deep scowl. "Took you long enough. Do you see the mess in the yard?"

The garden overflowed with cabbages, carrots, leeks, and onions. The stone well in the front yard vanished beneath a lush carpet of verdant foliage.

Margaret clenched her fists. "This is more than we can eat. If the monster keeps at it, we won't be able to step out of the house."

Bridget smirked, finding her sister's dramatic flair amusing. "Train little Lillian to control her earth gifts."

Ellen tipped her head, her curls bouncing. "It's your job. You're her mother."

Margaret's scowl sagged into a dispirited frown. "No. I fear she'll strangle me with a vine. She's evil."

Ellen burst into laughter. "Oh, dear. She's just a wee bit older than two."

Bridget placed her hands on her hips. "Ellen, we have to do everything in this family. Very well."

Ellen surveyed the abundance of vegetables and flowers in the garden. "Margaret, you could give the surplus to the townsfolk."

Margaret turned away, scowling. "Never. I'll sell it at my stall. At least I can make some money off the devil-child until you two get her under control." She retreated into the house, leaving the sisters to their own devices.

Moments later, Lillian darted out, her arms outstretched. Ellen embraced her niece and said, "You'll come to visit us for a while."

Bridget took hold of Lillian's hand, Ellen gripping the other. Together, they walked toward the gate.

Lillian halted, refusing to budge any further. "I have to say good-bye to my mommy."

Ean, Lillian's magpie familiar since birth, flew to the gate, cocking his head.

Bridget lifted Lillian into her arms. "Your mother knows. Don't worry about it." How long would Lillian continue loving her mother with the way she treated her? It was a constant source of frustration.

"I go by myself?"

Bridget chuckled while bouncing Lillian. "Yes."

"Not mommy?"

Ellen shook her head. "Mommy's in a bad mood. She has to stay home."

Lillian shook her head fast, her whole body squirming in Bridget's arms. "A bad mood all the time."

The aunts erupted in laughter, impeding their progress.

Lillian ceased her laughter, crossing her arms with a frown. "Why? She likes James and Grace better."

Bridget frowned, shaking her head. It was clear to everyone, even a young child like Lillian, that her mother showed favoritism. Margaret disregarded their advice to be kinder to her daughter, still holding her near-death experience during childbirth against her. She should be grateful she survived, since many mothers do not.

Ellen caressed Lillian's hair. "It's not your fault. It's the way she is."

Bridget winked at her sister, who she admired for her kind heart. She asked, "You like plants?"

Lillian beamed and lifted her shoulders. "Yes!" She stretched her arms out wide. "I watch them get bigger and bigger."

Ellen took Lillian's hand, smiling at her. "Then let's go to our house and tend to our garden."

The aunts led Lillian down the lane, taking turns carrying her since their home was over a mile away.

Lillian giggled each time they passed a stone wall along the road. Bridget noticed her niece coaxing the furze growing in the crevices to bloom.

Ean flitted from branch to branch, perching a moment to keep a watchful eye on the trio before taking flight again.

Bridget swung open the gate to their yard. "We're here. Now your lessons start."

Ellen placed Lillian on the soft green carpet of shamrocks covering the ground. Ean hopped alongside her.

Lillian gazed at her aunts, her head tilted. "What?"

Bridget entered the front door. "You're going to learn how to control your special gift, the one you have with all living things. Then you can return home." How she wished she could let Lillian stay here, in a loving environment free from scorn, but their home was too small.

They stood in their vibrant garden behind the small cottage, observing as Lillian toddled on her plump legs. The young girl's eyes shimmered with wonder as she explored the flowers and plants surrounding her, sometimes plucking a petal or leaf and bringing it to her nose to inhale. The flora flourished under her touch.

Bridget kneeled beside Lillian and whispered, "I want you to stop this flower from growing. It doesn't need to grow any further since it will wither away soon. Don't give too much. Close your eyes. Concentrate on that new sensation within you. Keep it to yourself."

Lillian closed her eyes. "Stay." She embraced herself. "It tingles."

"That feeling will fade as you grow older. It's a lot of energy for your small body. You did wonderfully. I'm proud of you." Bridget placed her hands on the ground, attempting to rise.

Ellen extended her hand to her sister, assisting her. "The ground seems farther away than usual. Now, Lillian, let's try something else before taking a break. Your aunts need to rest." She took Lillian's hand and led her along the row of flowers to a patch of bare soil. "Place your hands on this dirt."

Lillian plopped down and pressed her palms onto the earth's surface.

"Transfer some of your tingling energy to the seeds just beneath the surface. But only a little. Stop when you see the seedlings sprout."

Green shoots emerged before long.

Ellen noticed Lillian's hesitation as the sprouts continued to grow. "Remove your hands now."

Lillian frowned, lifting her hands and rubbing them together to brush off the soil. She stood and looked at Ellen. "I did bad?"

Ellen sighed and said, "You need more practice. You shouldn't make the plants grow too much. Only a little."

"Oh."

Bridget emerged from the back door, carrying a tray with tea and a small glass of milk. "Come along, you two. It's time for tea."

Ellen took hold of Lillian's hand. "And it's time for a well-deserved cookie, don't you think, Lillian?"

"Cookies! Then play flowers?"

Bridget glanced at Ellen. "Are we able to keep up with her?"

"I think she'll learn quickly. Tomorrow, we can teach her the names of the flowers. It'll be fun."

They enjoyed their tea, milk, and cookies, aware of the challenges that lay ahead. Lillian shouldn't have manifested her gift until she was older, around eight or nine years old. For now, it was about helping her gain control and imparting further knowledge as she grew older.

Using the practiced hand of a seasoned chore-doer, nine-year-old Lillian swept the kitchen floor, her motions smooth. The absence of the familiar crackling sounds from the stone fireplace alcove caught her attention, alerting her to the weakening fire. She hurried to the woodpile and retrieved a log, placing it on the dwindling flames. She waited for its dryness to ignite a new blaze.

To her dismay, the log erupted in a fiery explosion, unleashing flames in every direction. Lillian recoiled in shock, her arm bearing the painful mark of a burn. A scream of agony escaped her lips, provoking the fire to surge forth once more, devouring a nearby stool.

In a rush, Margaret, Lillian's mother, burst into the room, uttering a phrase in Gaelic that commanded the flames to retreat. Lillian, her brow furrowed, undeterred by the danger, grabbed a rag and battled the persistent flames. Sweat streamed over her face as she stamped out the burning embers that littered the floor.

Margaret's gaze bore into Lillian. She said through clenched teeth, "What happened here?"

Lillian squinted her eyes and thrust her chin out, meeting her mother's gaze. "I simply placed a log on the fire."

Margaret paced back and forth, her fists clenched. "This is a serious problem. How can this be? It must be the work of Morrigan. I am convinced of it." She pointed an accusatory finger at Grace, Lillian's older sister. "Go fetch your aunts."

Lillian rolled her eyes; her mother often blamed the Celtic Goddess for mishaps.

Grace pursed her lips, leaning away in defense. "Why are you yelling at me? It was her," she retorted, pointing an accusatory finger in Lillian's direction.

"Now!" Margaret's command pierced the air, urging Grace to leave in haste.

Turning her attention back to Lillian, Margaret stepped closer, her expression a mix of concern and frustration. "I knew from the moment you emerged from me, attempting to bring me harm, that you were an evil force. Nine years of proof, and now you possess two gifts."

Lillian grimaced, her eyes squinted, and her mouth twisted in response, her head tilting upward. "I don't understand why you persist in blaming me for that."

Margaret pointed toward the door. "Outside. I cannot risk you setting the house ablaze. Stay there until your aunts arrive." Under her breath, she muttered, "Faery-touched evil banshee."

Lillian marched out of the house, making her way to the sanctuary of the garden, her favorite refuge. Gathering a handful of large comfrey leaves, she shredded and pounded them on a nearby rock.

Using her finger, she applied the resulting green mush to her burn, giving gratitude to the plant with a touch of earth magick, bestowing energy for its growth.

Grace returned with Bridget and Ellen, breathless and panting. She cast a disdainful look at Lillian as she hurried into the house. Lillian's aunts approached her, their footsteps accompanied by disapproving clucks. Lillian hoped they would offer guidance rather than scolding.

Ellen's smile stretched from ear to ear. "Grace informed us you attempted to burn down the house. Another power, it seems?"

Bridget shook her head in disbelief. "Unprecedented in these times. You must tell us what happened. Leave nothing out."

Lillian recounted the events, explaining how she had placed a log on the fire and the ensuing chaos that unfolded.

Ellen nodded. "It seems we must hasten your education in controlling your fire gift. It is a formidable power, one that few witches possess. And to our knowledge, none have been blessed with more than a single gift."

Lillian leaned forward, her brows furrowed. "Fire gift? But I am an earth witch."

Ellen bounced on her toes, amusement dancing in her eyes. "You are both."

Bridget's expression turned solemn. "Keep this knowledge to yourself. Do not disclose it to anyone."

Lillian's countenance dropped. "Who would I tell?"

Bridget's lips twisted, her tone grave. "Consider it a warning."

Lillian recoiled from her aunts, rolling her eyes and emitting a snort. "Why is this happening to me? My mother already despises me, and now I possess two gifts. She called me a faery-touched evil banshee."

Ellen raised her shoulders in a sympathetic shrug. "Who can say? I wish I could assist you, but your mother is as obstinate as you are. Drochubh, drochéan." (A bad egg, a bad bird.)

Bridget tilted her head, rolling her eyes. "Your grandmother, Honoria, is also to blame. She said you'd be powerful and the biggest pain-in-the-arse for all of us," Bridget mimicked the voice of her mother. "Children born of that moon are that way because the Goddess Morrigan rules their fate." She nodded her head at Éan. "The magpie pecking at the window was an omen of back luck. It is so." She returned to her own voice. "And when she said 'it is so', it meant no argument. Honoria's word was the last word."

Lillian gave her aunt a half smile. "Mother's away with the faeries. How do I get back into the house?"

Ellen faced Lillian, her eyes twinkling, and the corners of her mouth turning into a fond smile. She patted Lillian's hands in hers. "We will get you under control before nightfall."

Bridget inhaled, holding her breath a moment before exhaling. She rocked on her heels. Her gaze focused on the ground as though searching for clues, like a seasoned detective. "It all depends on you—how much you desire to sleep in your own bed."

"Let us begin. I don't want to sleep in the barn," Lillian declared, positioning herself between her aunts and cracking her knuckles.

Under her aunts' careful tutelage, Lillian discovered the secrets of fire manipulation, feeling the heat of its power surge through her as she commanded it with a single phrase. They taught her the delicate art of drawing away heat from a fever, and providing warmth to those chilled. Above all, her aunts instilled in her the fundamental principle: "Do as you will, as long as you bring no harm." It was a mantra that echoed in her mind, guiding her every action as she honed her skills.

With the constant encouragement from her aunts, Lillian's confidence in her abilities grew. There was much to learn, a vast expanse of knowledge waiting to be explored, but she embraced the journey, knowing her aunts would be there every step of the way.

In the quiet moments of contemplation, Lillian wondered about the existence of other witches blessed with dual gifts like her.

Chapter Two

A DENSE FOG ENVELOPED the landscape as twelve-year-old Lillian ventured out of her home. She approached the well, hauling a hefty cast-iron pot for refilling, a chore she dreaded because of its weight.

Positioning the pot beside the well, Lillian grasped the rope fastened to the bucket and began its descent. Once the sound of the bucket splashing against the surface of the water reached her ears, she swung the rope to tip the bucket into the well. A gentle tug showed fullness, prompting her to turn the crank and hoist it back.

Unexpected splashing noises disrupted the tranquility. Lillian peered into the well, only to be greeted by a sudden eruption of water, drenching her and propelling the bucket and rope out onto the ground. As water gushed forth from the well, the water level rose and overflowed.

The force of the water propelled Lillian backward. Bewildered, she couldn't comprehend the reason behind this occurrence, but knew she would face her mother's wrath. Why did these mishaps always happen to her while her sister remained unscathed?

Water now posed a threat to the house. Lillian retrieved bags of cured manure from the garden to block the doorway's threshold. As she placed the last bag, her mother emerged from the house, only to stumble and fall into the water.

Lillian retreated, aware that her mother never missed an opportunity for corporal punishment.

"What have you done this time?" Her mother rose from the water, and Lillian swore she glimpsed her eyes turning red, accompanied by smoke wafting from her nostrils.

"I fetched water for soup." Lillian braced herself for her mother's strike, yet she refused to be bullied any longer. "Don't worry. I'll get help from my aunts myself!" She splashed away from the yard, leaving her mother to deal with the aftermath. As her aunts always said, 'Bad egg, bad bird.' Her mother despised that saying.

The serene stroll to her aunt's residence calmed Lillian's nerves, despite her damp and chilled state. "Tirim." Her dress dried, and the warmth was pleasant against her skin. "That's better." She glanced at Ean, soaring alongside her. "At least you remained dry."

The aunts would know what to do about her newfound water gift, and perhaps she could undergo training at their house. The prospect of time away from home was a treasure. She yearned to live there all the time, but alas, they lacked the space in their small cottage. But she knew they would welcome her for a short time.

Lillian unlatched the wooden gate covered in ivy sticking out everywhere. Ellen, an earth witch, didn't always keep it in check because of her fondness for plants. Several rabbits scurried away upon her arrival, while wrens hopped among the branches of shrubs and trees, seemingly unperturbed by the sudden company.

The front door bore a wreath fashioned from cedar boughs and wheat sheaves. Lillian waited, and soon Bridget swung open the door. As an air witch, Bridget possessed the ability to detect any change in the atmosphere, including a new individual in her vicinity. "What gift has manifested this time?"

Lillian shook her head, a sheepish smile spreading across her face. "Do you think I'd not pay a visit without reason? Water."

"Don't worry. We can help you. Come inside. We're eager to hear what happened and how furious our sister is." Bridget disappeared into the darkness.

Lillian stepped inside and closed the front door, allowing her eyes to adjust to the dimness. The outline of the kitchen table came into view, where her aunt Ellen chopped vegetables. Lillian took a seat and grabbed a knife to slice leeks, while Bridget placed a bowl of water in front of her.

"I hope you don't expect me to drink water like an animal."

Ellen giggled.

Bridget maintained a serious expression. "I want you to lift the water from the bowl."

"Oh." Lillian attempted to lift it, using only her thoughts. How should she approach this? She had learned to control her other gifts by focusing her mind on making things happen. Water. Wet. Smooth. Under her command, the water inside the bowl stirred. *How do I lift it?* She attempted to create waves, resulting in small ripples across the surface. Next, she tried to make the water splash. It felt ever so heavy. Beads of sweat formed on her forehead, causing her concentration to waver. "Ugh."

Lillian found herself alone in the kitchen. She pushed her chair back and stood. Through the kitchen window, she spotted her aunts tending to the garden, with Ellen slicing a carrot for the eager rabbits. She chuckled, realizing they all shared an affinity for creatures, even the despised fly.

The break quieted her mind, so she returned to the bowl of water. Her attempts seemed futile, as she only generated rolling waves sloshing against the sides. Frustrated, she slammed her hands on the table, causing the water to jump and her nostrils to flare. This time, the water rose, maintaining the same shape as the bowl. The sudden breakthrough caused her to lose focus once more. The water plummeted, splashing within the bowl and spilling onto the table. Lillian pushed the bowl off the table just as her aunts returned.

Ellen retrieved the bowl. "Are ye having fun?"

"No! I mean, I made the water rise, but only when I got angry."

"Tsk." Bridget tossed a towel at Lillian. "That's how you accomplish anything. You rely too much on anger—it dominates your emotions."

"It's difficult. A new gift means more work." Lillian wiped the spilled water from the table and floor before tossing the towel onto the table and plopping back into her chair. She looked from Bridget to Ellen. "May I stay here to work on it before returning home? Mother won't miss me."

Ellen replied, "Certainly. You're welcome here for a short while."

Bridget pursed her lips. "As long as you listen and follow our instructions. No magick that causes harm, absolutely."

"Of course. I understand. I'll do as you say, as long as I harm no one."

Bridget added, "Especially not your sister."

Lillian crossed her arms, her mouth down-turned. "You should experience being blown across a potato field by my beloved sister. It happens all the time, and nobody says a word."

Ellen said, "My sister raised her that way. But this is our way."

Lillian walked over to refill the bowl and returned to the table. "I'll do as you ask." She imagined her sister standing nearby, contemplating the possibility of lifting the water and drenching her. Splash. Her aunts jumped.

Bridget maintained a stern expression while Ellen chuckled. "I merely requested that you lift it, not douse us with a bath."

Lillian cleaned the mess once again, satisfied with the sudden progress. She would never expose her imagined intentions to her aunts, for they would send her away for violating their primary rule of doing no harm. If she focused her abilities on Grace, she would be successful. The vision in her head was forming water into droplets—they would make splendid weapons when frozen.

At fifteen years old, Lillian found herself in need of salt from the top shelf while preparing dinner. She stretched her arm as far as it could reach, but the elusive container remained out of her grasp. Determined, she pulled a chair from the nearby table. It collided against the counter before defying gravity, hovering a few inches above the floor. She exerted pressure, feeling the resistance give way as her frustration grew. With a forceful shove, the chair slipped out of her hands and soared through the air, hurtling back towards her. Reacting, Lillian ducked beneath the safety of the table to avoid the airborne furniture.

From her vantage point under the table, Lillian observed the surreal scene before her. The table and chairs floated, suspended a few inches off the ground. She exhaled in exasperation, contemplating the consequences of her newfound ability. What if she had been outside? She envisioned lifting the cow, disrupting its milk production from fright.

Another gift. This time Lillian decided against seeking help from her aunts. Determined to control her air gift herself, she focused her attention on a chair, willing it to descend to the floor.

"Lillian!" Her mother's voice rang out, slicing through the air, and in response, everything plummeted. Lillian spun around to face her mother, her anger simmering beneath the surface. "I have my air gift now," she declared. "How do you like that? Blame Morrigan, all you want. I don't care."

Grace entered the room, her eyes narrowed. Arms crossed, her bottom lip protruding, she unleashed her frustration. "Why is she getting all the gifts? She's not special."

Lillian faced her sister. "You're not special either. Help me set things right." She then turned to her mother. "After that, I will leave to visit my aunts for a few days. I'm sure they would welcome me. They appreciate my gifts."

"Great. I'll welcome the break," her mother said.

As the tension reached its peak, James, Lillian's older brother, arrived home from his job at the mill. Surprised by the chaotic scene before him, he looked at everyone. "Wow! What happened here?" He waited for a response. "Another secret? Fine. Want some help?"

A genuine smile spread across Lillian's face as she regarded her brother, the one person at home, who treated her with kindness. "I'd love it. Let our special sister stand there and watch." Her thoughts had already drifted towards the idea of leaving this place. Dublin sounded intriguing, offering the prospect of new experiences.

Margaret crossed her arms. "Lillian! Do not speak poorly of your sister. You should look up to her."

"Pfft." Dublin, it will be. She needed a map.

As she and James worked together to restore order in the room, Lillian's mind wandered to her future endeavors. She bid farewell to James upon completion of their task, promising to return in a few days.

On her favorite walk, she pondered whether there were any other gifts a witch could gain. Perhaps she already possessed them all. Lost in her thoughts, she contemplated how she could use her newfound abilities to make her mother and sister pay for years of torment. Grace, an air witch, took pleasure in tossing Lillian across the neighboring potato field, leaving her covered in dirt and potato greens sticking out in all directions. Lillian planned to return the favor, using her air gift to give Grace a taste of her own medicine.

Ean, her loyal companion, awaited her, perched on a nearby tree branch. Lillian wondered if it was possible to lift herself using her air gift. Although she had never seen Grace performing such a feat, Grace had dedicated little time to hone her air abilities. She only used her gift for nothing more than flirting and blowing Lillian away.

When she practiced encasing inanimate objects in water bubbles, Lillian harbored a secret wish to test her powers on a living creature. Grace would become her first target.

Upon reaching her aunt's house, Lillian heard laughter coming from the garden. Curiosity piqued, she followed the sounds and discovered her aunts enjoying tea amidst the serene setting. "What's so funny?" she asked, joining them.

Their gazes turned towards Lillian, warm smiles spreading across their faces. In this haven, unlike her home, only James wore a genuine smile for her. Bridget cast a knowing sidelong glance. "You've become an air witch now?"

Lillian nodded, her head tilted. "This time, I accidentally dropped the furniture. It seemed to work better when mother entered and scolded me."

Ellen's round face crinkled in thought. "Of course, dear. That is your way."

Bridget set down her cup, her expression serious. "We'll work on control, regardless of the emotion. Come, have a seat. You can practice using a teacup."

Lillian settled into a chair, her eyes fixed on the delicate teacup before her. Taking a deep breath, she focused her attention on the surrounding air, willing it to respond to her command. She envisioned a gentle breeze swirling around the cup, lifting it oh-so slightly off the saucer.

"Remember, Lillian," Bridget advised, her voice gentle yet firm, "the key to mastering your gift lies in harnessing your emotions and channeling them through intention."

Ellen chimed in, her tone encouraging. "Yes, dear. Embrace your emotions, but don't let them overpower you. Control is the key to unlocking the true potential of your air gift."

Lillian absorbed their words, her determination growing stronger. She focused on the teacup, envisioning invisible currents of air wrapping around it like a delicate embrace. The cup rose from the saucer, hovering in mid-air.

A mixture of awe and excitement filled the garden as Lillian saw the tangible manifestation of her newfound abilities. She guided the teacup in gentle arcs, testing her control and the limits of her influence over the surrounding air. The cup floated and moved, as if responding to her every thought.

Bridget and Ellen exchanged proud glances, their smiles widening. "Well done, dear," Bridget praised, her voice carrying a sense of admiration. "You possess great potential as an air witch."

Encouraged by her success, she considered the vast possibilities her gift could unlock. The world seemed more expansive, abounding in adventure and untapped power.

Her aunts, sensing her eagerness, shared knowing looks. "There is much for you to discover, Lillian," Ellen said. "The path of a witch is a journey of self-discovery, of unlocking the depths of your own magick."

Determined, Lillian pledged to embrace her training and learn to control her air gift, marked by precision and finesse. She knew her journey would not be without challenges, but she felt emboldened by the support of her aunts and the promise of a wider witching world.

As the sun began its descent, casting a warm golden glow over the garden, Lillian made a silent vow to herself. She would continue to grow and harness her gifts, not only to seek retribution against her tormentors but also to forge her own path and shape her destiny as a witch.

Chapter Three

Seventeen-year-old Lillian and her sister Grace meandered home, Lillian pulling the handcart. Their mother, Margaret, had set off to administer a folk remedy at a customer's home. Grace, ever eager to mock her younger sibling, maintained an unusual silence while Lillian reveled in the tranquility.

Amidst their stroll, Lillian's gaze rested upon her cherished trees and plants, while she weaved dreams of a future where she would wed or seek work in Dublin. She yearned for the day she would leave her family behind. The mystery of her father's departure lingered in her thoughts, a topic her mother attributed to Lillian's alleged wickedness—a lie that Lillian dismissed, for he had left before her birth, before he could know.

The sound of swift, weighty footsteps drew nearer from behind, and a strapping young man, fiery red hair tied up in twine, drew alongside, his steps slowing in sync with theirs. He greeted them with a smile. "Dia duit!"

His god was not one they revered, but that was their shared secret. If they dared, they might whisper "Bandiais duit," a phrase that might summon the authorities to their doorstep, for most of Ireland belonged to the Church of Ireland. The church had silenced the worship of goddesses and pagan ways, relegating them to clandestine rituals.

Lillian's heart skipped a beat. She had encountered no one as beautiful as he. The gorgeous red hair and eyes, the green of a blade of grass, held her in thrall.

The young man halted.

Grace, bolder than most, fluttered her lashes and teased, "Did my sister's face startle you? Fear not, I'll shield you from her."

"I'm Sean. Sean Maguire. Here, let me take that." He grasped the cart's handle, relieving Lillian.

Grace leaned in, invading his personal space. "I'm Grace. The most sought-after catch in Manorhamilton. Just ask anyone."

Lillian rolled her eyes before she said in her quietest voice, "I'm Lillian."

Grace chuckled. "My sister is the most fearsome in Manorhamilton."

Sean countered, "I doubt that. She doesn't seem scary at all."

"You'll see. Never say I didn't warn you."

Grace's brazen flirting caused Lillian's face to redden. She had never encountered someone that stunning, and she struggled not to stare. They walked together for a while, Grace chattering away and Sean stealing glances at Lillian, who hesitated to speak, consumed by trepidation.

Sean did not seem perturbed by Ean, her magpie flitting from fence posts to tree limbs beside them. In Ireland, everyone dreaded encountering a solitary magpie, a harbinger of misfortune, unless greeted. But Sean did not offer a greeting to Ean.

Not aware of her setting, Lillian went by her treasured elderberry tree, its majestic appearance not catching her eye since she was so absorbed in her new companion..

As they arrived at their home's gate, Sean relinquished the cart back to Lillian, who wished their walk could have been longer. Their gazes locked.

Grace shot Lillian an icy stare. "Come on, Lillian. Cease making a fool of yourself."

Sean turned to leave. "Slán leat."

Grace tugged at the cart, striving to seize Lillian's attention. "Stop daydreaming. You can only dream of catching a man like that. You're destined for a life of solitude." She sneered at Lillian. "That's the price of being born wicked. Put the cart away." Grace stormed off, her hair bouncing on her shoulders.

Lillian bit her tongue as she stowed the cart and guided the cow into the barn. Any outburst would only invite her mother's wrath, and she would be consigned to sleep beside the cow—her mother's favored punishment, even if it were just for Lillian's existence.

As fate would have it, Lillian's path would cross with Sean's on several more occasions, but Grace seemed resolute in her mission to lay claim to the handsome young man.

Lillian filled a wicker basket composed of teas for fever, sleep, and to calm, her movements swift and practiced. After a week of incessant rain, the sun now blazed, the air muggy and oppressive. It matched her mother's foul mood. Lillian's survival strategy involved keeping her head low and her mouth shut to avoid drawing attention.

"Lillian! Where is your sister?" Her mother's voice pierced through the thick air, sharp and authoritative.

Feigning ignorance, Lillian raised her eyebrows and shrugged her shoulders. "I don't know."

"Go find her." The words left no room for negotiation, a firm command.

Lillian suppressed the urge to roll her eyes or sigh, knowing such insolence would only result in a slap across her face, leaving an embarrassing red mark on display for all to see. Stepping out of the booth, she welcomed the temporary reprieve from her mother's scrutinizing gaze.

The market's main road intersected with several others, and Lillian set off, checking both directions at each cross street. Her gaze fell upon her sister, Grace, leaning on Sean in front of the blacksmith's shop. Heat rushed to Lillian's cheeks as tears threatened to spill. Why did Grace always seem to get everything, leaving nothing for her? And now she had also captured Sean's attention. Dublin seemed more appealing with each passing day. If only Lillian could find her way there.

Lillian couldn't understand. She was certain he was interested in her. Or was it all just teasing? For the first time, someone showed her any attention. Perhaps she had misinterpreted the signals. How would she be sure if he liked her? Such was her life.

She moved in their direction, but her feet felt heavy, as if resisting her will. Sean's head turned, and their eyes met, but before she uttered a word, he was gone. Determined not to let Grace slip away, Lillian quickened her pace, intent on closing in on her. "Mother told me to find you!" she shouted, striving to mask her hurt and frustration.

Grace sneered, cocking her head and waving her hand in a dismissive manner. "And you have." Twirling, shoulders back and hair flung, Grace began her practiced snub.

Lillian followed close by, calculating her words to avoid providing Grace any ammunition that would land her in trouble. "You have to work at the booth," she said, matching Grace's stride. "I'm going to keep an eye on you."

"Go ahead," Grace replied before breaking into a run. When she reached a street that led to their booth, she pivoted and sprinted, followed by Lillian in hot pursuit.

Lillian, the superior runner, shook her head, realizing the futility of Grace's endeavor. No way Grace would elude her grasp. Together, they arrived at the booth, Grace gasping for breath while Lillian resumed her task unfazed.

She seethed, a boiling cauldron of suppressed anger, ready to erupt at any moment. The image of Grace and Sean together seared into her mind, wondering if he found her unattractive or too quiet compared to Grace's incessant chatter. Despite the urge to break down in tears, Lillian refused to show any vulnerability in the presence of her mother and sister.

Grace recounted her chance upon Sean to their mother, each word delivering a blow to Lillian's already bruised ego. A weight settled upon her chest, and she struggled to ignore it. Ean, her familiar, swooped over from his perch above Grace's head, snatching a few strands of hair in his beak. Grace yelped and reached for the top of her head. "Ow! Get that wretched bird away from me!"

Lillian suppressed a laugh while the conversation shifted to Grace's hatred for Ean and her unfortunate lack of a familiar. Yet, the knot in Lillian's stomach and the weight on her chest persisted, leaving her uncertain about what steps to take next.

CHAPTER FOUR

SEAN RACED TOWARDS HIS tiny hut, more like a lean-to, on his employer's vast farmland. The weight of his conflicting emotions came crushing down on him. He shut the door behind him. The resounding thud and sound of the latch closing gave him a sense of temporary comfort. Collapsing onto his solitary chair, he found himself ensnared in a web of thoughts revolving around Lillian and Grace.

How had things spiraled out of control when Grace appeared out of the blue at the blacksmith? Though his feelings for Lillian had grown, Grace's persistent advances had proven difficult to resist. The internal turmoil tore at his heart, demanding resolution. It was time to set things right.

He squeezed his eyes shut, covering his face with his hands. The hurt in Lillian's eyes when she caught Grace's shameless displays of affection on him tore his heart in two. The undeniable allure of Grace ignited a certain fire within him. But, most of all, he yearned for Lillian's company, her presence resonated a longing he couldn't ignore any more.

Sean knew that to build a future, he needed to rise above his humble beginnings. He dreamed of providing for a family and offering them all the comforts and stability. The thought of working for another farmer the rest of his days filled him with dread. He wanted a life worth living, a sheep farm of his own.

Restlessness consumed him, causing him to pace back and forth within the confines of his humble hut. His thoughts raced like untamed stallions, galloping through the vast expanse of his mind. The time had come for a decision, one that would shape the course of their intertwined lives. Should he be honest, laying bare the depths of his inner struggle, risking the loss of Lillian? Or should he continue on the way things are while grappling with his own turbulent emotions?

The weight of this internal conflict was unbearable. He needed to confront the truth, no matter how formidable it may prove to be. With a steadying breath, he steeled his resolve and charted the course of action that would define their future.

Sean envisioned a life with Lillian by his side, raising a family together, perhaps even running a small sheep farm of their own. He could see them teaching their children the value of hard work, honesty, and kindness, shaping them into the finest citizens. And with Grace, he imagined a life of excitement and unpredictability, where passion would fuel their days and nights.

He closed his weary eyes, allowing his focus to settle on the rhythmic cadence of his breathing as he sunk back into the worn contours of his chair. Sean would navigate the labyrinth of his feelings, his heart leading the way, and hope for the best.

Sean rose from the chair, summoning his courage to embark on the journey that would bring him to the doorstep of Grace and Lillian's shared home. He realized that to make his dreams a reality, he must first confront his feelings and make a choice.

He raced down the road until he found himself at their front door. He braced himself. His knuckles rapped against the wood. The sound echoed like a warning of the hard conversations coming.

Lillian sat at the worn wooden table, her gaze fixed on the stew in her bowl. She pushed the spoon through the thick broth, the weight of her emotions making it difficult to swallow. How could Sean do this to her? The lump in her throat seemed insurmountable, threatening to choke her with every bite.

Her mother's words echoed in her mind, giving room for doubt and resignation to permeate. Maybe there was truth to her mother's warnings. Maybe there would be no one for her, and she would end up like her spinster Aunt Bridget.

The tension in the room tightened as Grace announced, "Mother, Sean is going to be my husband." Lillian's downcast eyes lifted, observing her sister's animated gestures and the way her voice rose. "We are so compatible. You won't believe how handsome he is."

Margaret, their mother, interrupted, "Does he have money?" Her words cut through the air, a stark reminder of the practicality that often governed their lives.

Before Grace could respond, a sharp knock reverberated through the room, drawing their attention to the door. Grace made haste to answer it. Lillian turned in her chair, curiosity replacing her despondence as she sought to see the unexpected visitor.

As Grace laid eyes on Sean, her demeanor transformed. Her hand reached to primp her hair, and a radiant smile graced her face.

Sean's voice cut through the room, searching for Lillian amidst the commotion. "Is Lillian here?" His inquiry held a note of urgency, pulling everyone's attention toward him.

Grace tilted her head, her lashes fluttering as she batted her eyes. "No, but I am," she replied, a hint of triumph in her voice.

Lillian's heart pounded within her chest as she scrambled to the door, an instinctual need to assert her presence. "I'm home," she announced. Pushing Grace aside, she stepped out, meeting Sean's gaze. "Hi. I missed seeing you today."

The tension between the sisters became palpable, hanging in the air like a storm waiting to break. The smile on Grace's face faded into a scowl, her disappointment clear as she slammed the door behind Lillian's departure.

Sean, unaware of the turmoil brewing inside the house, explained himself. "My boss had me run an errand for him in the opposite direction from town." His words held an apologetic tone, as if seeking understanding and forgiveness for the circumstances that led to his delayed arrival.

The front door opened. Margaret, hands planted on her hips, took a step forward, her eyes narrowed. "You will not talk to her unchaperoned. What are your intentions?"

Sean approached Margaret, his tone earnest as if to assuage her concerns. "I'm sorry, but I do not mean to offend. But I like your daughter very much." His words carried a genuine sincerity.

Margaret rubbed her chin as she glanced behind her, searching for answers within the house, before focusing her attention back on the young man. "Which daughter?" Her question hung in the air, suspended between hope and uncertainty.

"Lillian," Sean responded, leaving no room for doubt. Margaret's gaze met his unwavering choice, shifting from him to her other daughter. The realization hit her, prompting a mixture of shock and realization to sweep across her face. "You're not marrying Grace? Did you change your mind?" Her accusatory tone pierced the room, the weight of disappointment pressing on her.

Lillian watched the exchange, her arms crossed over her chest, her brows furrowed. "Figures you'd say that," she muttered under her breath, defiance lacing her words.

"Get in here young man and explain yourself." Margaret said before disappearing inside.

As Sean extended his arm, a gesture of respect and admiration, Lillian's heart swelled. No one had ever treated her with such reverence, making her feel deserving of respect and love. At that moment, she made a silent vow to herself. If he asked, she would marry him.

The scene shifted, the setting transforming into the dark night. Lillian, fueled by anger and a wish for retribution, made her way to put the cow in her pen. She ensured the safety of the animal, her actions almost mechanical as her mind remained fixated on the recent events.

Upon returning to the house, Grace stood at the door, blocking Lillian. A sudden gust of wind spiraled around Lillian, propelling her across the field, tumbling. Anger flared within her, fueling her determination to confront Grace.

Lillian struggled to regain her footing, dirt clinging to her clothes and hair as she stormed into the house. Margaret had rushed to console Grace, leaving Lillian unnoticed as she seized the opportunity to slip into her mother's room. She was determined to have her grandmother's trinity pendant. Lillian had always sensed its presence, her connection to her family's history driving her to have it. Without a sound, she retrieved the necklace, tucking it into her pocket.

A mischievous plan took shape in Lillian's mind, an act of defiance against her sister's cruel actions. Dozens of frogs materialized in Grace's bed, a playful yet pointed retaliation against her tormentor. The room erupted into chaos as Grace screamed, frogs hopping in every direction.

Her mother's voice rang out, a stern command. "Lillian, stop this instance!" The weight of her mother's disapproval hung in the air, an obstacle that threatened to overshadow Lillian's sense of justice.

Unyielding, Lillian stood her ground, her voice defiant. "I will not. She unleashed a wind storm to send me across the field again. You say nothing about her using her gift on me. She started it because she is jealous. You're mad he doesn't want her, only me, who you only tolerate because it violates the main tenet of 'do what you will, as long as it harms none.'" The bitterness and frustration found a voice. Storming off, Lillian left the chaos behind, finding solace in the quiet shelter of the barn, where she would bed down for the night.

Morning arrived, casting a new light on the unfolding drama. Lillian's belongings lay by the barn in a basket, a stark reminder of her position in the family hierarchy. Grateful for the small mercy, she realized the basket that held her belongings was one she had crafted for her mother. It pained her to see her heartfelt creation returned.

Ean's search for shiny objects ended without success. He flew to the railing. Lillian watched as her fingers clutched the trinity pendant hidden in her pocket, a symbol of her grandmother's strength and power.

She knew, deep within her soul, that this necklace held secrets and potential beyond her comprehension. The precious trinity pendant, adorned with a ruby, an emerald, and a sapphire in each of its three lobes, carried a whispered legend of untold power. Lillian resolved to keep it safe, hidden away in the barn where her mother and Grace would never think to look.

Standing at the gate, Lillian awaited her mother's arrival, prepared to walk with her to the booth. But when Margaret emerged, accompanied by a distraught and swollen-eyed Grace, the atmosphere grew tense once more. Her mother's words sliced through the air, sharp and final. "You don't work for me anymore. You need to find a job to pay for your lodging in the barn." Margaret curled her lip and wrinkled her nose.

As her mother passed by, a dismissive snort escaped Margaret's lips. Grace's glare and raised eyebrow spoke volumes, reflecting the divide between the sisters.

Chapter Five

Now what am I going to do? Lillian's lips formed a tight pinch as she contemplated her predicament, her hand rubbing the tense muscles at the back of her neck. In her mind, a forbidden fantasy played out, where she encased her mother and Grace in a watery prison, drowning in their own misguided actions. The anger burned within her, fueled by the unfair punishment she endured for Grace's self-inflicted humiliation. Her mother's favoritism was a bitter pill to swallow, her affections extended to everyone but her youngest daughter.

Resting against the weathered gate, Lillian's fingers grazed the worn wood as she pondered her next move. With a flick of her wrist, she released the essence of the frog spell, sensing its fading power dissipate into the surrounding air. Her attention then shifted back to Grace's bed, a focal point for her brewing revenge. She focused her mind on the fibers that composed the ropes, visualizing them growing pliant and loose, mirroring the looseness of Grace's deceitful lips. She surged her energy into the spell, Lillian's determination tightened, the ropes succumbing to her silent command.

Her brother James emerged from the door, pausing at the gate. His voice carried a mix of concern and amusement. "You really made them mad this time. You should have heard them last night."

A weary sigh escaped Lillian's lips. "Been kicked out. I have to get a job to pay to sleep in the barn."

A sympathetic glimmer shone in James' eyes as he extended his hand, offering a lifeline amidst the chaos. "We can use a hand at the mill. Come. I'm not mad at you. It would do you some good to get away from them for a while." His outstretched hand remained unanswered, but Lillian walked past him without a word, her silent acceptance of his support clear.

"You're probably right. Maybe I'll get married and get away for good."

A hint of sadness tinged James' voice as he replied, "Aw, but I'll miss you. You keep the house interesting. They keep blaming you for everything and miss checking themselves." James slowed his pace, allowing Lillian to not fall behind as they embarked on the path to the large linen mill on the outskirts of town.

When they approached the mill, James received a warm reception from his fellow workers, their greetings affirming his popularity. It impressed her how well-liked he was among his peers.

Stepping through the mill's entrance, Lillian attempted to navigate the bustling environment, her eyes locked on James' guiding figure. "A quick tour first," he explained, "then I'll take you to the order keeper's office where they need help."

The sights and sounds of the spinning wheels mesmerized Lillian as the workers tended to the raw flax fibers, transforming them into delicate threads. The air hung heavy with a swirling tapestry of suspended particles, adding to the mystique of the bustling mill. They moved past rows of spinning wheels until a set of stairs led them to an upper floor, where the clatter of many looms created a deafening symphony. Lillian marveled at the sheer scale of the operation, the scent of oil and grease permeating the air. On James' signal, they descended back downstairs, leaving the cacophony behind.

In a spacious office near the mill's entrance, Lillian found herself amidst a collection of wooden desks and chairs. Only one desk was occupied, where a young man worked on a pile of papers. At the central desk, a woman with light brown hair fashioned in a bun glanced up, a welcoming smile gracing her lips. "What brings you to see me, James?"

James led Lillian to the woman's desk. "I brought my sister, Lillian, to give you a hand, Hannah. Are you interested?"

Hannah's eyes widened in relief as she surveyed the piles of papers surrounding her. "Oh my, you know it. All these orders have been spinning my head, even infiltrating my dreams. I'm so far behind." She directed her gaze toward Lillian. "Are you willing to learn?"

A determined smile formed on Lillian's lips, determined to make a positive impression and prove herself to her brother. "Yes. What do you want me to do to help you?"

Hannah raised an eyebrow, her pencil poised. In a swift motion, she slid a ledger across the desk's surface. "You can start by recording these orders," she pointed to a stack of papers, "into this ledger. I believe you can figure it out. If not, ask. Choose a desk."

Lillian nodded, grasping a stack of papers, and moved toward the nearest desk. Peering back at James, she winked and mouthed a silent "thanks."

Her brother placed the ledger on the desk, his protective nature clear as he lifted his sack. "I'll share my lunch since you have nothing. Can't have you starving on your first day."

Hannah observed the exchange. "That's sweet. James is such a kind soul. We are lucky to have him." Before turning her attention back to her mountain of paperwork, she smiled at Lillian. "Now, let's get to work. We have quite a lot to accomplish."

As the door closed behind James, Lillian watched him vanish into the bustling mill, rows of looms stretching out before him. A small sense of comfort washed over her as she spied Ean, her faithful familiar, perched at a window behind Hannah's desk. Determined, Lillian opened the ledger, the columns aligning just right on the accompanying paperwork. The task at hand might be monotonous, but it was what she had to do to pay to sleep on the hay.

When the resonating blare of a horn echoed through the mill, signaling the end of the day's toil, Lillian remained steadfast at her desk, determined to complete the order she had been recording. She glanced up from her task, her eyes alit as she spotted James approaching. A warm smile graced her lips. "I'm putting the finishing touches on this order, and then I'll be ready."

James eased himself onto the corner of her desk. Lillian closed the ledger, placing the completed order atop her stack, a sense of accomplishment swelling within her. It was her first venture into a world beyond her mother's humble folk remedy booth. "I'm all set now. Goodbye, Hannah."

Hannah paused in her own work, acknowledging Lillian with a farewell nod. "Goodbye, Lillian. Impressive work on those completions. If you could hand me your ledger, I double-check the new hires' entries for a few days. So don't fret about it."

Lillian's brows furrowed, her smile unwavering. "Oh, it's alright. I feel confident in what I've done." She picked up the ledger and made her way over to Hannah's desk.

Hannah gestured towards a spot on her desk. "Just set it there. I'll see you in the morning. Have a pleasant evening."

Lillian placed the ledger as instructed, returning the smile bestowed upon her by her newfound boss. Comparing working under Hannah's guidance to her mother's realm was akin to contrasting a soaring hawk to a humble handsaw. She cast a knowing glance at James. "Shall we?" They strolled out of the mill, joining the small group of stragglers, as the bulk of the workforce had already departed.

The homeward road offered a picturesque vista. The majestic Dartry Mountain loomed in the distance, its rugged peaks forming a breathtaking backdrop against the verdant expanse of the valley. Lillian never grew weary of the enchanting beauty that enveloped the landscape. Hedgerows and stone walls flanked the dusty path they traversed, demarcating the boundaries of lush fields and pastures. Amidst the serene ambience, the melodic symphony of birdsong mingled over the sporadic bleating of sheep and the lowing of cattle from nearby meadows.

James broke the silence when he asked, "How was your first day?"

Lillian pondered for a moment. "The work may be monotonous, but I must admit, I rather enjoyed it. Not a soul raised their voice at me all day, which is a rare occurrence unless I'm visiting our aunts."

"It's a good place to work," James said.

"I realized today that I don't quite know what you do there," Lillian remarked, curiosity brimming in her eyes.

A faint smile tugged at the corners of James' lips. "I'm the fixer. I tend to all the equipment."

As they continued their path, Lillian's gaze fell upon Sean, who walked a way ahead. "Sean! Would you mind waiting for us?" When she received no response, she turned to James. "My voice doesn't carry far. Would you please?"

James turned to Lillian, a reassuring nod stressing his response. He cupped his hands around his mouth to project his voice toward Sean. "Sean!"

Sean pivoted on his heel, a smile illuminating his face as he waved in acknowledgment. He came to a halt, awaiting their approach.

Lillian and James quickened their pace until they reached Sean. Together, they embarked on the rest of their journey, walking side by side. Lillian frowned as she said, "It's not wise for you to call on me at home. Mother and Grace are still in an uproar over yesterday." She resolved to keep her temporary dwelling in the barn a secret.

Sean shook his head. "I'm sorry for causing such a row for you. Perhaps we can meet somewhere else?"

James raised his index finger. "There's a magnificent willow tree by the river Shannon, its branches cascading to the ground."

Lillian arched an eyebrow, nodding in agreement. "That's a splendid choice indeed. Sean, do you know where that is?"

"Aye, I do," Sean nodded. "Now we only need to decide on a time."

Lillian shrugged her shoulders, a sense of liberation enveloping her words. "How about after work on Fridays? I'm sure no one will miss me for one day a week."

That evening, Lillian moved her meager possessions to the loft, transforming a few hay bales into a makeshift bed. If she were to call the barn her home, she was determined to make it as habitable as possible. When she descended the ladder, James startled her, bearing a plate of food. She hopped off the bottom of the ladder. "Thank you. That's awfully kind of you. I'll need my first paycheck before I can afford any food. Although I gathered some greens from the garden." She accepted the plate from James and motioned for him to take a seat.

James shook his head. "I snuck this out. I should probably make my way back before any suspicions arise, at least until those two calm down in a few days."

Lillian pursed her lips in understanding, nodding in acknowledgment. "You do what you must. Goodnight."

James waved as he turned and made his way back into the house.

After she finished her meal, Lillian found herself confronted by Bridget and Ellen standing in the barn's doorway.

Even in the dim evening light, Lillian saw Bridget's brow furrowed and lips pressed together. Bridget said, hands on her hips, "You know well what we've taught you. 'Do as you will, but harm none.' Yet, you employed your magick against your sister, causing distress to both her and your mother."

Lillian tilted her head to the side, contemplating their words. "Why does that principle only seem to apply to me? Grace frequently employs her gift of wind to blow me across the potato field, and nobody bats an eye. Yet, the moment I send a few frogs her way, I find myself banished to this place." She gestured around the barn, encompassing the hay-strewn ground. "That was the first time I ever used my abilities against her."

Ellen let out a weary sigh. "Life, my dear, is often unjust. We taught you, not Grace. True, it would have been preferable for Grace to receive the same guidance."

Bridget turned away, leaving behind a bittersweet farewell. "We can no longer offer you guidance. You must find your own path. Good luck." Ellen followed her sister's lead, both exiting the barn, their departure leaving a lingering sting of rejection.

Lillian felt the sharp pang of their abandonment. Even they, who had been her guiding lights, had now turned their backs on her, intensifying the ache within her. The mistreatment she endured from her mother and sister, adding their ultimate rejection, fanned the flames of rage that swirled within her. It threatened to spill over, tempting her to succumb to its consuming embrace.

Yet, amidst the turmoil, she found solace in James, Sean, and Ean. Though her circle may be small, it remained unbreakable, a sanctuary she could always rely on.

Chapter Six

On a Friday afternoon, Lillian stood beneath the sheltering branches of a magnificent willow tree that stretched out along the Shannon River. Her heart pounded from a mix of excitement and apprehension. The customs dictated that a young woman should never be seen alone with a man, but Lillian defied these conventions. She cared little for the rules imposed by a church that had suppressed the ancient pagan ways of her country for centuries.

As she waited for Sean to arrive, a whirlwind of thoughts swept through Lillian's mind. What if he didn't show? What if he had changed his mind about her and chosen Grace instead? The prospect of such rejection loomed large, and she wondered what it was about her that repelled people, even her own family.

The memory of her recent misdeed haunted her. She had sent frogs to Grace's bed, an act of mischief she had never engaged in. Yet, growing up, her mother and sister labeled her as wicked. The cruel words she endured daily had fueled her own fantasies of ill intent towards Grace. Did that make her evil?

Lost in her contemplation, Lillian gazed at the flowing river next to the sturdy tree trunk. Tears welled in her eyes, blurring her vision like a gathering storm, threatening to overflow like a waterfall down her cheeks.

"Lillian."

Startled by the sound of her name, she spun around to find Sean standing before her, a figure divine. In that moment, all thoughts of loneliness, rejection, and evil dissipated into thin air. "Sean, I feared you wouldn't come. Perhaps you reconsidered."

"My boss kept me busy at work. It was torment. Bad timing," Sean explained, making his way towards her. "People would wag their tongues if they caught sight of us like this."

Lillian tilted her head, shrugging one shoulder. "I couldn't care less."

"Haha, me neither." Sean pulled her into a warm embrace.

Lillian's heart raced, and she wondering if Sean could hear its thunderous beat. But there, another heart pounded against hers, synchronized, beating in unison. She leaned into his embrace, enveloped by a sense of euphoria she had never experienced before. It was pure bliss, and she yearned to feel this way always.

Sean pulled back, his hands still on her shoulders, his eyes locked on hers.

Lillian realized how little she knew about Sean, despite finding herself in his arms. It was time to rectify that. "Tell me everything about yourself. Where are you from? What is your family like? What are your likes and dislikes?"

Sean chuckled. "That should have come before the hug, shouldn't it? Why don't we sit beneath this magnificent willow, and I'll regale you with the tale of Sean?" He took her hand and led her to a nearby spot.

Lillian followed suit, sitting beside him. As she gazed into his eyes, it was as if she peered into his very soul.

Sean leaned back, his head against the tree trunk. "Well, I hail from Drumshanbo, near the southern tip of Lough Allen. My entire family toils at the Creevlea iron works. I despised it. All I ever wanted was to work outdoors, among animals. So, I left. My father has never forgiven me for it." He offered Lillian a half-smile, tinged with sadness.

Lillian detected the pain hidden in Sean's eyes. His family held great importance to him, unlike her own. She remained silent, waiting for him to continue. When a minute or two passed without further words, she prompted, "Do you aspire to have your own sheep farm?"

"Aye, that would be grand."

"I wish to know you better, but you're not making it easy for me. You remain a mystery," Lillian said, her curiosity piqued.

Sean sighed. "You'll have a lifetime to unravel the mystery that is me. It doesn't all have to happen today."

Lillian nodded, a slight smile playing on her lips. "You're right. I should head home. It's not advisable to walk unaccompanied at night." She rose and brushed off her skirt.

Sean stood, taking her hand and giving it a gentle kiss.

A blush crept onto Lillian's cheeks, causing her to forget any words or actions. She pulled away, turned, and made her way towards the road.

Sean hurried to catch up. "I'll see you on Monday, on our way home."

"Yes, you will. I'm a working girl now," Lillian said. As they reached the point where they would part ways, a heavy sigh hung in the air. "Goodbye, Sean."

"Slán leat." Sean jogged off.

Lillian took her time walking home, her mind swirling. It vexed her he had evaded her questions, yet she couldn't deny the thrill of seeing him again. She already realized how much she would miss him over the weekend.

Monday arrived, and James accompanied Lillian on their journey home. Sean caught up with them, having finished his day at the sheep farm. Giddiness filled Lillian, as the weekend had dragged for her.

Sean voiced his yearning. "Is there any way we can meet over the weekend? Waiting until Monday to see you again is unbearable."

Lillian stroked her arm and leaned towards Sean. "The weekend *was* unbearable to me as well. Now that I have no obligations, I'm free to escape. My only task is taking care of the cow, milking her in the morning, grazing her in the pasture, and bringing her back in the evening. That leaves us with plenty of time."

"How about I prepare a picnic for you on Saturday? Bring a blanket," Sean suggested with a beaming smile.

James said, "I suppose there's no room for a third wheel. I'm joking, of course."

Lillian jabbed at her brother. "Knowing you, you might just appear out of the blue."

"Nah, I won't intrude on your love," James replied, chuckling.

Lillian saw Sean six days a week and wondered why he wouldn't see her on Sundays. After all, his church service only lasted in the morning. However, she refrained from prying, content with the time they spent together.

One Saturday, Sean fidgeted, wringing his hands and patting his pocket several times. Lillian wondered what was going on, but he would reveal it when he was ready. So she waited. After they finished their meal, Lillian packed the basket, and Sean took hold of her shoulders.

"I have something to ask you."

Did I do something wrong? Is this it? Is he going to reject me now? Lillian's heart raced, and she swallowed hard. "What is it?"

Sean kneeled on one knee before her. "I kneel before you like a knight, vowing to protect and serve my lady. Will you marry me? Become my wife?"

Lillian's hands flew to her cheeks, tears welling. She had hoped they would marry one day, but she hadn't expected it so soon. "Yes, yes, of course! Yes!"

He leaped, lifting her off the ground and spinning her around, giving her a tight embrace and a lingering, passionate kiss.

Lillian pulled away when the heat became overwhelming, and she struggled to catch her breath. "And now?"

"Now we plan a wedding," Sean declared.

Lillian shook her head. "We can't afford a lavish wedding. And where will we live?"

Sean shrugged. "My place on the farm is too small. I can barely turn around in there. But I've been saving my money, so maybe we can find a place. That will be my responsibility."

Lillian walked towards the road, her head bowed, treading through the grass and wildflowers. "We'll also need to find someone to marry us. I'm not a member of any church, so that might pose a problem. One of James' friend is a Protestant pastor; perhaps he would officiate. I'll have James ask. And what about your family? Will they attend?"

Lillian noticed a shadow cross Sean's face, and she waited for his response. He hadn't spoken about his family in weeks.

"I wrote to them about us and asked for their blessing. I didn't receive it. They insist I return home and marry a local girl," Sean confessed, his voice tinged with sadness.

Lillian stood by Sean's side, looking at him. "I only have James, and he supports us. So I'll have him by my side."

"You won't tell your mother and Grace? They'll find out eventually," Sean questioned, concern etched on his face.

Lillian crossed her arms. "I won't speak to them."

A month later, Lillian and Sean stood facing each other, reciting their vows under the shade of the large willow tree. The only witnesses was James. After the pastor pronounced them husband and wife, they sealed the moment with a tender kiss. Sean whispered in Lillian's ear, "I have a surprise for you."

"What is it?" Lillian asked, anticipation coursing through her.

Sean's grin widened from ear to ear. "We're going for a walk. Come, hold my hand. We're married now, and no one can stop us."

They strolled along the road towards Lillian's former home, passing it by after bidding James farewell. Lillian wondered why they were heading in that direction. They reached the outskirts of town and turned the corner to a secluded lane until they arrived at a small thatched roof stone house.

Sean scooped Lillian up, ensuring she wouldn't trip, and opened the door. "I can't have you stumbling and bringing bad luck upon us."

Lillian noted there was no threshold to stumble over, as the floor was made of packed earth. "I thought it was to make it seem like I don't want to consummate the marriage."

Sean stepped inside the house, placing her on the ground. "It doesn't matter. This is our new home. Together. What do you think?"

Lillian twirled around, taking in every detail. A fireplace, a table, chairs, and a small room in the back containing a bed and a chest. It was small, but it was their own space, a significant improvement from the barn. It was a closer walk for her to the mill, but a longer one for Sean to the sheep farm. Overwhelmed with gratitude, she hugged Sean. "It's perfect. Thank you, my love."

Sean's shoulders slumped as he let out a heavy sigh. "I was afraid you wouldn't be pleased. It's all I could afford."

A knock interrupted their conversation, and Sean went to answer the door. James stood there, holding a basket filled with Lillian's belongings. Sean took the basket from him and placed it on the table. "Come in, James. Stay and chat for a while."

James hesitated, glancing at Lillian for reassurance. "Are you sure? I can come back another time."

Lillian walked to James and pulled him inside. "You're always welcome here, anytime. Do you think Mother or Grace will notice I'm gone?"

James settled in the chair Sean offered, a pensive expression on his face. "Probably not for a while. I'll have to deny any knowledge to protect myself."

Sean's face grew serious, his eyes widening. "I don't blame you. Your mother seems like she can be quite harsh."

Lillian interjected, her voice firm. "She can be even worse, if you can believe it. But let's not dwell on them. I wish I could offer you something, but I'll be using my pay to buy food."

James smiled. "I received my pay as well. How about I treat you both to dinner and drinks at the pub? Consider it a celebration to kick off your married life."

Sean furrowed his brow, placing his hand on the table. "Are you sure about that?"

"It sounds like a wonderful way to start your new journey together. A pint to loosen up and enjoy the evening," James gave a playful wink.

The rhythms of married life embraced Lillian's soul, an enchanting symphony of shared moments with Sean. They spent every waking hour together, a tapestry woven with threads of purest joy. It was a harmony she had never dared to dream of.

Touched by the celestial hand of fate, a blessing arrived as a baby girl. Stella, the epitome of innocence, graced their lives. Lillian, fueled by a desire to shield her from the shadows of her own past, devoted herself to her daughter's care. She would not allow the mistakes of her own mother to tarnish the precious bond they shared.

Stella blossomed into a gentle soul, her silence a testament to her goodness. In the tender years of her youth, she discovered her gift—air magick — a power inherited from her ancestral lineage of witches. Lillian taught Stella to use her ability only when she was around, keeping her daughter's abilities hidden from view. The lessons took root, and harmony prevailed. Stella's interests soon intertwined with her mother's craft, her curiosity ignited by the herbs Lillian gathered and the alchemical wonders she wove.

As Stella's tiny feet grew stronger, allowing her to travel the short path to the marketplace, Lillian found herself compelled to contribute to their family's finances. Armed with a basket brimming with her healing concoctions, she embarked on the journey to face the ghosts of her past—her mother and sister. It was a choice not out of obligation, but a wish to forge a brighter future.

Lillian arrived at the marketplace to discover her mother's booth was empty, replaced by whispers of her ailing condition. Urgency gripped Lillian, her remedies finding swift purchase among the worried townsfolk.

With Stella's small hand clasped in her own, Lillian retraced the path of her childhood, sharing fragments of nostalgia as they approached the threshold of her old home. The familiar trees and shrubs evoked a bittersweet smile, but doubts sowed seeds of hesitation within her. Why was she here, facing the cruel phantom of her mother's disdain? But Lillian resolved to teach Stella the sanctity of the high road, a guiding light amidst the shadows. She rapped on the door, her pulse quickening.

Grace, her sister, answered, her silence betraying an ocean of unspoken grievances.

Lillian said, "I came to give my regards to Mother."

Grace admitted Lillian, casting a glare like a moonless night. Within the confines of her mother's chamber, Lillian offered her presence as an olive branch. "Ma, I came to see you. Do you want to meet your granddaughter, Stella?"

Her mother, a specter of fading life, possessed a voice barely audible but still venomous. "No. Leave. I don't want to see you. Curses to your next child."

The words pierced Lillian's heart, a venomous sting of rejection. Hope had faltered in the face of unyielding animosity. Yet, knowing this marked their last farewell, she summoned the strength to embrace the high road. "May your end be peaceful. I love you." She turned to exit, only to be confronted by the imposing figures of her two aunts. "Excuse me."

The aunts escorted Lillian away from her mother's room, their gazes filled with the weight of past grievances. Bridget's voice dripped with scorn. "Why are you here? Your sister still wrestles with nightmares of frogs."

Lillian chuckled, her laughter a soft caress in the air. "I came to give my mother a blessing, that she may find peace in her last hours. As for my sister, that chapter is long closed."

Ellen rolled her eyes. "And how fares your married life? Many believed you would never find love, destined to toil in the ceaseless storms of strife and worry."

"Opinions, like whispers on the wind, surround me at every turn. But I cherish the life I have. A life blessed with an extraordinary husband and a daughter who fills my heart with joy. Is that strife and worry?"

Lillian caught Ellen's horrified expression, her eyes drawn to the necklace adorning Lillian's neck. A knowing smile tugged at Lillian's lips, aware of the silent wishes her aunts harbored—to cast their mother's necklace, a resplendent silver trinity knot of sapphire, ruby, and emerald, into the depths of the sea. Their mother, her grandmother, had wielded it with callous intent, heedless of the cost to others. The tenet to cause no harm was a foreign concept, lost amidst her quest for personal gain.

As Lillian neared the gate, the echo of Bridget's words reached her ears. "She better not torment her sister." Lillian's laughter danced on the breeze, a melody of liberation. Her sister had been the architect of torment throughout their shared childhood.

As she walked away from her childhood home, Lillian vowed never to return, severing the tethers that bound her to a life steeped in anguish.

Months passed, and Lillian gave birth, the screaming bundle placed within her arms. She extended the child toward Sean, expecting warmth and tenderness to envelop their growing family. Instead, he recoiled, shaking his head in disbelief. "Don't you want to hold your child?"

He retreated further, his head still shaking. "I sensed it the moment you were with child. Something is amiss. Lillian, evil emanates from her."

Desperation coursed through Lillian's veins. "What if we name her Mary? Would that alter your perception?"

A shrug, broad shoulders carrying the weight of uncertainty. "A name is but a whisper. It does not shape the essence of the beast."

Lillian's glare pierced through the swirling tempest of their discord. "She is not a beast. It is the church's poisoned whispers that taint your senses." Memories of her family branding her as evil at her own birth resurfaced, the cruel legacy she had never escaped. Now, her husband had cast the same shadow upon their daughter. Lillian clung to her mother's final words, echoing in her mind. Was her child cursed? No more so than she herself was inherently evil. Evil demanded action, and no one would dare brand her youngest daughter.

Yet, Mary's cries persisted, an incessant symphony of distress that consumed the days and nights. Lillian employed lavender waters, tinctures, and sachets in her desperate quest for solace. Moments of respite would fleetingly grace their lives before chaos shattered the fragile peace. She pondered seeking her aunts' guidance, but the memory of their last time together dissuaded her. In the community, no other healers held sway, leaving her to trust that this phase too shall pass, and tranquility would reclaim their lives.

She shielded Mary from Sean, a shield fashioned from her fierce love. His accusing words, questioning her loyalty and doubting the provenance of their child's cries, struck her soul with twin blades of pain. Lillian never looked upon another man with the depth of affection as she did Sean. And their daughter was no banshee, no harbinger of ill fortune. In her fervent prayers to Morrigan, Lillian beseeched the goddess to embrace Mary's being, soothing her cries and unveiling a contented existence.

The symphony of their lives played on, its melody a delicate balance between the shadows of the past and the light of an uncertain future.

CHAPTER SEVEN

LILLIAN'S EYES DARTED FROM one side of the bustling row of wooden stalls to the other. She took in the vibrant array of fruits and vegetables, the smell of spun wool, and the sight of stacked blankets all displayed under colorful awnings. The aroma of fresh bread wafted past her, tempting her to stop at the baker's booth, but she pushed past it determined. She heard the vendors hollering and the clink of money being exchanged. Lillian ignored it all until she reached the butcher's, where she came to buy pork as a treat for Sean.

Lillian noticed Grace wasn't working their mother's old booth next to the butcher's. Grace had taken it over after their mother's passing.

Lillian clenched her jaw as Mik, the butcher, glared at her. His massive frame towered over her. He could slash a pig or a cow with a single swing of his knife. His customers had to endure his scorn, as no competition existed in town.

Undeterred, Lillian asked over the cries of Mary, "Where's Grace?"

Mik snorted. "Closed. No rent, no booth."

Lillian raised an eyebrow. "Interesting. Are you going to help me?"

Mik sneered as he threw a dismissive hand at her. "I thought you were just being nosy about your sister. She disowned you, I hear."

It figured Grace badmouthed her to anyone who would listen. "No. I disowned her. Only my brother can sit at my table. What do you have today?"

"Shoulder meat."

"I'll take 4 ounces. And not all fat. It's for Sean."

After paying for her purchase, Lillian hoisted Mary in her swaddle sling and took Stella's hand. She made haste through the market towards the center of town. Stella asked, "Where are we going now?"

Lillian's mind raced, and she forgot her usual restrictions of a small child in tow. She noticed Stella couldn't keep up with her; Lillian tempered her pace. "The magistrate."

They arrived at the magistrate's office and entered. She had never had business inside. She always waited outside when her mother went in. The office was nicer than anything she had seen in Manorhamilton. Beautiful paintings hung on the walls; the furniture, not ones made in town.

Lillian recognized the woman in the outer office as one of her best customers when her mother was too sick to sell remedies in her booth.

"I want to talk to the magistrate about renting my mother's old booth," Lillian said.

The woman frowned. "It's your sister's right now. She's behind on rent, so she may not use it until she brings the rent current."

"But I'm family, too. Since my sister is behind, she has no way to pay for it, I'm sure. I want to rent it."

The woman rose from her chair. "Let me ask what he wants to do. Wait here." She entered the office and closed the door.

It tempted Lillian to barge into the office and address the magistrate herself, but she knew she had to play by the rules. The woman emerged and shook her head. "He won't. Your sister has time to fix her delinquency."

Lillian rolled her eyes. "That will not happen. Grace has no business sense." Her sister didn't even have what it took to practice her air magick to do more than blow Lillian across a potato field. She doubted she could learn how to run the booth.

Lillian, no longer bothered by the rules of the office now, marched in, her heels clicking against the hardwood floors, Stella in tow. "I will bring the rent current."

"What are you doing in my office? You don't have an appointment!" Ross O'Brien, a short man with red curly hair, dropped a sizable chunk of bread dripping into butter and jam. Since his appointment as magistrate, his waistband had doubled. Now Lillian saw why.

"I want that booth as I am my mother's daughter, as much as Grace," Lillian said as she hoisted Mary in her sling. "Grace has failed. I can show you. You see me selling in town every day."

Ross placed one hand on his desk and leaned forward. "I have said what I have said. No!"

Lillian asked, "So when?"

Ross raised his voice. "What?"

Lillian looked at Stella and stroked her hair. "When will you give me a chance?"

"Why do you think you should have the booth?" Ross asked.

Lillian stiffened her posture, her sharp eyes scrutinizing the man. "Where are your other healers? A town needs a true healer." She arched an eyebrow, her lips set in a firm line. "Grace is not that healer."

Ross leaned back in his chair, his expression inscrutable. "Healer," he mused, stroking his chin. "Yes, you are correct. If Grace cannot raise the funds by the end of the month, I shall grant your request at the start of the next." He waved a dismissive hand. "Now, leave my office. And in the future, make an appointment."

Lillian inclined her head, a hint of contrition in her voice, eyeing his unfinished bread. "I apologize for my impertinence and hope I didn't cause you any trouble." As she made her way out of the room, Stella followed.

When they emerged into the bright sunlight, Stella queried, "Where are we going now?"

"Home," Lillian replied. "I must prepare a wonderful meal for your father." She needed to explain her plans, and his favorite foods always made things easier to swallow.

The next month, Lillian received permission to sell her remedies in the booth instead of her basket. Now she had baskets of lavender, sage, and peppermint, the smells intoxicating to anyone within several feet. The townsfolk eager to part with their coins put her in profit in a few days.

After a week of running her new booth, Mik, the butcher in the next booth, slammed his hand on her counter, causing Mary's scream to echo through the marketplace. Customers and vendors stopped what they were doing and turned toward Lillian's booth. Stella burrowed into Lillian's skirt. Lillian snapped her head to the butcher. "What do you want that's so urgent you have to make my baby cry harder and scare Stella?"

The butcher glared at her, pulling his head closer, lips drawn tight. "Make her stop! I can't listen to another day of it. All day long. I can't even hear my customers."

Lillian took a deep breath, trying to keep her cool. "How can you say that? She's a mere baby. I can't change her temperament anymore than your wife can change yours."

He tilted his head, jutting his large chin out, a hard smile slid across his face. "Humph. Maybe I'll go to the magistrate. That brat's howling and your damned magpie is chasing my customers away."

Lillian saw his hand slide along her counter as he left. She pulled the moisture from the wood in front of his hand, causing the small pieces of wood grain to rise and break. No one got away with treating her children ill.

"Ow!" The butcher grabbed his hand, examining it. He turned to Lillian. "You don't even take care of your booth. What if a customer got a splinter?"

Lillian smiled, lifted her chin, exposing her slender neck. "I have a poultice to remove it. I would gladly help them." She returned to finishing her preparations for the day, fuming about the confrontation. *That man is grumpy day after day, like a dark cloud over him all the time. And he expects Mary to stop crying.* She realized then what to do. A way to show the butcher how he is.

She spun around and raised her voice enough to make sure Mik could hear her over Mary's bellows. "You might be right. Mary cries

like a waterfall, hard and loud. I'll try some lavender water."
Mary loved lavender water, though it had a short-term effect on
her.

Lillian spoke a spell under her breath, a hand on her grandmother's necklace.

By elements of water, air, and thought,
I cast a spell, with intentions sought.
A rain cloud dark, I summon thee,
To follow this person wherever they be.
When foul thoughts arise within their mind,
Let rain pour down, a truth unkind.
With each negative thought, they dare to think,
Let water fall, as the cloud shall wink.
So mote it be!

A puff of cloud appeared above his head. "Yeah, try that."
Turning away, the cloud released rain on his bald head. He
swatted over his head, looking up at the clear blue sky. As he
moved to get away, the cloud followed. Nostrils flared while the
butcher held his elbows wide, hands on his hips. Rain fell harder.

The soaked butcher spent the day cutting meat and helping
customers. When anyone asked about the rain cloud, he shouted
back, "Get out of here!" A puddle formed where he worked,
getting larger until his footsteps made waves as he moved within
his booth. He closed early.

Lillian watched as the rain cloud followed him. She wondered
when he would realize he had to change his outlook to make
the cloud stop sopping his bald head. He had a wonderful life, a
lovely wife, and a pleasant house.

Ean did his part by defecating on Mik's counter. He squawked and hopped to the back of Lillian's booth, perched on a box where he spent most of his day watching over Lillian and the girls.

Lillian squinted, eyes lit with a twinkle of mischief. She held Mary close. "That's what he gets for complaining about my little one." She figured the adage her aunts taught her to do no harm didn't apply if someone harmed her or her family.

Chapter Eight

Lillian tended to a man with a terrible cough, her hands moving skillfully as she mixed the ingredients for the tincture. In the meantime, the magistrate strutted over to her booth, puffing out his chest to seem more imposing despite his burgeoning stomach.

"Good morning, Magistrate. How can I help you today? Is someone sick?"

He leaned in, lowering his head to stare through squinted eyes. "How did you create that cloud over Mik's head?"

Lillian stepped back, taken aback by the sudden accusation. True, she gave Mik a rain cloud, but that somebody would come right out and accuse her was a surprise. "Magistrate, I am a healer, not a cloud maker. Are you saying I control the weather? Quite absurd."

The magistrate rolled his eyes in response. "You need to stop your games. Your sister warned me about you."

Lillian groaned and forced herself to rein in her anger before she told him off. "Grace envies me. I have Sean and now she's perturbed she failed at selling remedies."

The magistrate's tone turned menacing. "If you cause any trouble for the other vendors, I will end your lease. Keep your child quiet...," he pointed at Ean, "and do something about that bird. He follows you around and no one wants to introduce themselves all day. A solitary magpie is very disturbing." He departed into the crowd.

Lillian discerned a foreboding settle in her stomach as the magistrate walked away. As much as she hated to, she spelled Mary's mouth shut, as her mother did to her often. "Ean, stay here on top of this box. I can't afford to lose my lease." Spooked by a raven or magpie because of a rhyme was absurd, but that was the reality of it.

The magistrate's words echoed in Lillian's mind as she continued working, trying to ignore the growing knot in her stomach. Any misstep would cost her the booth that had become savings for Sean to buy his own sheep farm.

The longer the day went on, the more Lillian felt like she was being watched. The other vendors whispered and cast her furtive glances, and even the customers appeared to avoid her booth. She tried to focus on preparing more remedies, but her mind kept drifting back to the magistrate's warning. She had caught wind that Grace had been spreading lies about how she made men swoon over her. Now it appeared she told everyone that Lillian was a witch who controlled the weather. And the magistrate seemed to take stock in it.

As the day drew to a close, Lillian breathed a sigh of relief that she had made it through without further incident. She gathered her belongings before making her way home. She walked, Stella sang to herself, Mary cried, and Ean flew alongside them.

As she headed home, she thought about the magistrate's brother, known for his cruelty and vicious temper, who used his brother's power to his advantage. Lillian understood the risks of revenge, yet the thought of getting back at the magistrate was appealing. But she wouldn't target the magistrate himself; his brother would be the perfect target. She derived satisfaction at the idea of striking back, but she deemed patience was key. Revenge should be served cold, like the icy winds that blew from the mountains in the dead of winter.

A week later, Lillian found Sean home early, his presence a welcome surprise. "My love, you're home early."

"Aye, and for no good reason. I hope you're prepared to take a walk," Sean said. He paced back and forth in front of the crackling fireplace, his restless energy palpable. "Everyone's talking about that strange cloud that follows Mik, dumping rain on him even in his own house. And they always raise your name. Did you have a falling out?"

Lillian narrowed her eyes as she weighed her response. She took a deep breath, attempting to keep her composure. "He wants Mary to stop crying. He's grumpy. Perhaps he's offended a faery?"

Sean scoffed. "Stop it! Faeries don't exist. And Mary cries a lot. I know."

A sudden surge of warmth coursed through Lillian's veins, igniting a fire within her. She pressed her lips together, her brows furrowing. "They exist as much as your god does. And you - a father should be on your child's side." She was careful to hide her magick from Sean but never considered the rain cloud would break her.

Sean's voice reverberated through the house. "We're moving out of town. If we have less of a presence here, the gossip will die down."

"But I don't want to move," Lillian protested.

Sean softened his tone, his pacing coming to a halt. "Trust me, you'll love this house." He spread his arms wide. "It offers more space, and you'll finally have room for a proper garden instead of constantly scouring for herbs."

"Fine, but I want to see it before I agree," Lillian said.

"Let's go then," Sean replied.

Lillian made sure Mary remained snug in her swaddle sling, ready for the outing. They lived near the market, in a small and rundown house. But it suited them for saving money for something better later. She figured at least another year or two.

As they embarked on the long walk, exhaustion from the day's work took its toll on Lillian. The picturesque view that unfolded before them reinvigorated her spirits. Benbo mountain, with its craggy peaks and lush greenery, stood as a majestic backdrop. The family crossed the meandering Bonet River multiple times before arriving at the serene banks of the Shanvaus River. A charming, thatched-roof stone house stood before them, captivating Lillian's heart at first sight. She caught herself planning what to plant where. She bounded off the stone path to peer through a window, imagining the possibilities that lay within.

Sean produced a key from his pocket. "You can get a better view this way."

Lillian gave him a quizzical glance. "Why do you have a key?" she asked, suppressing any anger that threatened to surface. The allure of the house had overshadowed her emotions.

"I wanted you to have a better view." Sean unlocked the door, stepping aside to allow his wife to enter.

Lillian crossed the threshold, Stella's innocent gaze fixed on Sean as she followed her mother into their potential new home. Natural light, streaming through windows that boasted actual glass, bathed the room. Gone would be the days of drafts and chilly breezes invading their living space. Lillian's eyes were drawn to the magnificent stone fireplace positioned on the far wall to her left. The kitchen area housed a sturdy table and chairs, the stone floor beneath her feet replacing the dirt of their current dwelling. An exhilarating surge of adrenaline coursed through Lillian's veins, infusing her with newfound energy.

To the right, two doors beckoned her curiosity. Lillian approached the first, grasping the worn wooden handle. As she swung the door open, a spacious bedroom greeted her, complete with a cozy bed and ample shelves for storage. She lingered, taking in the space, before proceeding to the next door. Behind it, a smaller bedroom, a perfect sanctuary for Stella. Excitement welled within Lillian's chest, her heart full of joy.

Stepping back outside, Lillian surveyed the rest of the property. "Look at that! A root cellar! We didn't even have one at my family's house," she exclaimed.

A small, dilapidated barn caught Sean's attention. "I'll fix it up and get a cow for fresh milk. We can even raise a pig to sell to the butcher," he said, unaware of the discomfort the word 'butcher' caused Lillian. She realized the extra money would go towards the higher rent for such a lovely place.

Strolling amidst the abundant garden space, Lillian's mind had visions of flourishing vegetables, fragrant herbs, and vibrant flowers. She contemplated how she would harness her powers to nurture a new garden.

Sean brought a temporary halt to her excitement. "But," he said.

Lillian's shoulders slumped, anticipating a smothering of her enthusiasm. Bracing herself, she prepared for the potential disappointment that awaited her. "Yes?"

"The major problem is the well. It refills slowly, meaning we must use water wisely," Sean said, shaking his head. "It's hard to believe, considering we're at the base of a mountain. One would expect runoff to replenish it."

Lillian smiled at her husband, her mind already planning solutions. As a water-witch, she possessed the ability to rectify the issue. For the time being, she held her tongue, to not appear too eager. Instead, she asked a practical question, "Can we afford it?"

To her surprise, Sean chuckled. "This house has remained vacant for far too long. The landlord struck a deal. I'll handle the repairs, and you transform the grounds into a thing of beauty. The rent is the same as it was in town. We just have to walk further to work."

Lillian couldn't help but feel a twinge of hurt at the realization that Sean had decided without her. Yet, she masked her emotions behind a half-hearted grin. "You already settled this, haven't you? It hurts that you excluded me from such significant decisions. But the walk holds its charms."

As she turned to head toward the barn, tears threatened to well in Lillian's eyes. Why did men always treat women as inferior? If only Sean could understand the power she possessed and the lengths she went to conceal it.

Stella, catching sight of a rabbit, chased it across the yard, interrupted her thoughts. "Stella, let the rabbit be. We must always respect nature," Lillian admonished her daughter.

Stella looked toward Sean, seeking his approval. When he shook his head, she slumped her shoulders and hung her head.

Lillian turned to face her family once more, her heart heavy. "I'm ready to go home. I have work to do," she announced. She strode off, her mind already buzzing with plans for their new home and the potential it held.

As they retraced their steps, Lillian couldn't help but reflect on the challenges that lay ahead. In a world where men often dismissed women, she found solace in her hidden powers that coursed through her veins. The journey home gave Lillian a chance to catch her breath and mentally prepare for what lay ahead.

Under the shimmering glow of the full moon, as midnight loomed near, Lillian slipped out of bed, her movements careful. The dying fire in the hearth called for attention, and she added a log, coaxing the remaining embers with the poker until the flames rekindled. She slung her bag of prepared supplies in hand and readied herself for the night's endeavor.

Little by little, Lillian turned the front door handle, ensuring no sound disrupted Sean's peaceful slumber. The cool night air enveloped her as she ventured forth, guided by the moon's ethereal radiance. She traversed the winding road and crossed a tranquil river, arriving at the two-story stone and timber-framed house of the magistrate's brother.

Lillian grappled with her decision to direct her retribution towards the magistrate's brother instead of the magistrate himself. She realized that attacking the magistrate might lead to more attention on her after she was accused of causing Mik's rain cloud because of their argument about Mary's crying. She sought vengeance on someone close to him, realizing the unbreakable bond between the brothers and their intertwined lives..

Seeking cover, she nestled behind a bush, her fingers brushing against its prickly leaves, finding solace in its concealment. Despite her hidden vantage point, she could still watch the scene unfold. Nearby, Ean, her ever-watchful companion, perched on a fence post, his head tilted.

Lillian dropped the bag on the ground and crouched beside it, the shadows of the bush casting an enveloping darkness. Her hands searched until they found the energy emanating from two stones—Jet and Labradorite.

The black stone, Jet, a powerful ally for harnessing the earth's energies on the spiritual plane, rested within Lillian's palm. The Labradorite cabochon, a gift from her aunt Bridget, possessed the ability to work within the natural laws, allowing her to manifest her desires. In the moonlight, shades of blue, gray, and green iridescence shimmered from one stone while the other appeared as a void.

From her bag, Lillian retrieved a sachet containing crushed rue and blackthorn leaves, placing the stones within its confines. While facing the house, her gaze fixed upon it, she rolled the stones together within the pouch, the fragrance of the crushed herbs mingling in the air. She raised the bag high in front of her as she spoke the incantation:

Through the hearth, the bats will come, disturb the air and vanish.

The chain of bats is unending until the light of the half moon is finished.

Let two brothers fight to extinguish, then blame each other.

So mote it be!

A gust of wind erupted from the pouch, swirling and twisting upon itself, a miniature tornado in her hands. Lillian's hair danced around her face, yet she held steadfast, unwilling to release the enchanted bag. The conjured wind grew in strength and magnitude, propelled by the force of her spell, until it soared toward the house, slipping down the chimney.

Lillian smiled as she closed the pouch and nestled it back into her bag, which she slung over her shoulder. She brushed her hair away from her face.

Stepping onto the worn dirt road that led to the house, Lillian inched closer to the window, craving a more intimate view of the scene within. As her eyes scanned the windows, a flicker of wings caught her attention. She released a long sigh. Her spell had indeed worked its enchantment, a testament to her tireless efforts over the past months to refine and perfect her creation spell.

The choice of bats held a deeper significance for Lillian. Symbols of transformation and rebirth, they embodied the very essence of change in life—an essence needed by the magistrate's brother. It was a poetic choice, a gentle nudge from the forces of nature to inspire a shift in the brother's manners, guiding him towards a path of growth and enlightenment.

Ean fluttered towards the window, peeking inside. He flew back, hopping on the ground at Lillian's feet. She spoke in a reassuring whisper, "Don't worry, Ean. Everything is fine."

Though weariness weighed upon her, Lillian hurried, eager to return home. It would prove challenging to explain her late-night absence. Once inside, she sought solace by the warmth of the fireplace, allowing the fire's gentle embrace to dispel the chill that clung to her skin. She slipped back into bed, grateful that Sean remained undisturbed by her clandestine endeavors.

CHAPTER NINE

LILLIAN FOUND SOLACE IN the enchanting beauty of the Glenade valley as she embarked on the homeward trek with her precious daughters. The lush greenery and babbling streams provided a comforting backdrop to their journey, their steps light and carefree. Little Mary toddled along, her joyful cherubic face beaming until she grew tired and screamed her displeasure. Stella delighted in counting the birds and plants that adorned the vibrant landscape.

Ean, Lillian's loyal magpie familiar, soared through the air, his ebony feathers shimmering in the sunlight. Travelers they encountered along the road would salute or greet the magpie. Lillian and her girls would giggle at the encounter, their laughter filling the air like a joyous melody. They often recited the whimsical rhyme, "*One for sorrow, two for mirth, three for a funeral, and four for a birth.*"

Ean had always been a source of solace and protection for Lillian, his companionship bringing comfort and strength in the face of adversity. She dispatched him on errands to fetch things for her spells or check if Sean had finished work. He watched over her children with unwavering vigilance. No one wished to be swooped by a magpie, as they were fierce defenders of their nests. Lillian couldn't help but cherish their bond, grateful for his unwavering presence in her life.

As they approached their beloved cottage, nestled at the edge of the Glenade valley, Lillian's heart swelled. The thatched roof and stone walls exuded a timeless charm, the embodiment of a cherished home. Lush blooms adorned the garden, their vibrant colors breathing life into the surroundings. A stone fence encircled the front, its weathered appearance adding a touch of rustic allure.

Yet, amidst her tranquility at her home, the rumors of bats fluttering out of the O'Brien's hearth pervaded the town. The rumors painted a picture of an eerie phenomenon, casting a veil of intrigue and mystery over their community. The talk of the town about the bats was rather amusing. They flew into the house but did not appear to have entered through any openings. If they opened a door or window, the bats flew out but never seen outside.

The townsfolk may have linked the bat incident and the rain cloud over the butcher, which occurred almost two years ago, with the magistrate's warning. However, she knew better than to let idle gossip tarnish her spirit. After all, who did they turn to when they needed healing?

Still, were the bats too obvious? Perhaps she should have opted for a more commonplace occurrence, like a hundred rabbits hopping about in the garden. With her extraordinary powers, anything less than the extraordinary would be a disappointment.

Upon her arrival home, Lillian's gaze fell upon the cart Sean built. Sean's intent remained shrouded in mystery, and she couldn't help but hope that it signified a new venture, a departure from his labor at the sheep farm. Her heart fluttered, eager to uncover the secret.

As she approached their cherished cottage, the tension in the air crackled, casting a palpable unease over their reunion. Sean's voice sliced through the stillness. "We need to have a conversation, and then you will have a lot to do."

"What troubles you?" Lillian asked. "Why have you returned early from work?"

A heavy sigh escaped Sean's lips, his weariness etched upon his face. "Rumors about you again. This time it's about bats. Last time it was a rain cloud following the butcher, even in his shop and home. Before that, it was frogs. The magistrate came by a few days ago when you went to Lough Glenade to gather herbs. He asked many questions and said he wanted to talk to you personally. He asked me if you were a witch." The weight of the word 'witch' hung in the air, its venomous sting poisoning the atmosphere. Sean's frustration erupted, his fiery locks cascading as he threw his head back in exasperation.

A flicker of disappointment etched across Lillian's face, her lips curling into a pout. "I spoke with him," she said. "He did not accuse me of witchery. Instead, I enlightened him. How could a healer be responsible for such occurrences?" She paused, contemplating how best to assuage Sean's concerns. The opinions of others influencing him appeared to her as a fruitless endeavor, a futile dance that only led to wasted time. "He said nothing about me being a witch."

As their eyes met, Lillian's heart plummeted into an abyss of despair. Scan's features twisted into a mask of accusation. The words escaped his lips like venomous arrows that seemed to pierce through the air. "Are you out of your mind?"

Lillian fought to maintain composure, her teeth sinking into her lower lip to contain her own tumultuous emotions. She knew she could not reveal the truth, the depths of her actions and the convictions that propelled her forward. No, Sean could never know the extent of her involvement.

"I am not crazy," she uttered, her voice barely a whisper. "I stand firm knowing that I have done nothing wrong."

Lillian clung to her beliefs, refusing to reveal the truth to Sean. The truth was hers to bear alone, a burden she accepted in the name of safeguarding their love and their family's future.

Sean strode to the cart, his voice carrying a sense of determination. "I've secured a house near Carrick-on-Shannon," he declared, his words hanging in the air like a decree. "My aunt's husband passed, and she will move in with my sister. The landlord has agreed to rent the house to us. We shall depart at the break of dawn tomorrow. Begin packing."

Lillian felt a surge of anger rise within her, bile seeping into every fiber of her being. How dare Sean make such a decision without consulting her, without considering her feelings? The audacity stung like a venomous arrow, pricking at her pride. "Just like that, you uproot us, swayed by idle gossip," she said. "People revel in their incessant gossip, finding excitement in the mundane. You made me move before, but at least you had the courtesy to discuss it, even if it was a mere semblance of a conversation. I adore this home, our community, and the income I earn in town."

Sean strode into the house, only to reemerge carrying the girls' bed, placing it upon the cart. The weight of his actions, both physical and symbolic, hung heavy in the air. "Perhaps next time, I shall leave alone," he said. "I don't see you packing."

Lillian's mouth dropped open, her heart shrunk from Sean's callous attitude, right in front of their daughters. She fought to suppress her swirling emotions, knowing that changing his stubborn mind would prove futile; his resolve overshadowed her own.

Taking the girls' hands, she marched into the house. She retrieved a sturdy burlap bag from the bottom drawer of the dining room hutch, its worn fibers hinting at years of use and hidden treasures. "Stella, Mary, gather two of your favorite items and pack them in this bag. We can't bring everything. The cart is too small."

Just as the mention of the cart escaped her lips, Sean materialized, his presence casting a shadow over the moment. "The cart is the right size for the horse to pull and the new house's size. It's not large, and you probably won't approve, but we didn't have time to be finicky. We need to put some distance between us and the whispering tongues."

Lillian held her chin high, her slender neck exposed. With a steady, lower-pitched voice, she said, "That's your decision, not mine. I'm not running away, tail tucked between my legs."

Removing herself, she set her sights on the kitchen. Her thoughts drifted to the bustling town of Carrick-on-Shannon. In her day-dreams, she envisioned a thriving business with her remedies sought after by eager customers. As her hands moved to pack the kitchen essentials, her excitement pulsed through her veins, lending a swift-ness to her actions.

Lillian stepped into the bedroom. Sean, absorbed in his own packing, paid her no mind, his actions speaking volumes of his disregard. Lillian, trying to seem unperturbed by his indifference, shrugged and gathered her own belongings.

In the bedroom next door, the girls sat engrossed in their own world of play, their innocent laughter filling the room. Lillian walked over to their door, stood for a moment to watch. "I asked you to pack, my loves," she interjected, her voice a tender reminder of their pending departure.

Stella, her eyes gleaming, looked up. "It's so hard, Mama. I love everything I have," she said. Mary, echoing her sister's sentiments, nodded in agreement.

Lillian kneeled, enfolding the girls in a warm embrace, her arms a sanctuary of comfort. "I understand, my darlings. It is difficult to choose when everything holds a special place in our hearts," she said. "But for our new adventure, I ask that you select two of your most cherished possessions. We'll make space for them on our journey."

Stella's gaze drifted towards the empty expanse in their room that once cradled their bed, and leaned into Lillian. "Where will we sleep, Mama? Da took our bed," she asked.

A playful sparkle ignited in Lillian's eyes as she engaged in a game of tickles, eliciting giggles from Stella and Mary. "Fear not, my precious ones," she reassured them, her grin spreading. "You'll sleep in our bed."

Stella and Mary's enthusiasm filled the room, their little bodies bouncing. "Yay!"

"Now, my dears, time to choose your two most beloved treasures," Lillian reminded them, her words a gentle nudge towards decision-making.

Mary, a mischievous twinkle in her eye, clutched the kitten that had slipped into the room. "One," she proclaimed, her love for the feline surpassing all others.

Lillian, aware of Mary's unwavering affection for her constant companion, nodded in understanding. "Very well, my little one," she said. "Our furry friend will come along, offering its vigilant service as our trusted mouser in our new home."

Lillian made her way into the kitchen, the aroma of baked bread and the distinct scent of dried fish enveloping the room. She prepared a simple yet nourishing supper, a feast born of love and resilience. Once she set the table, she summoned Stella and Mary, their giggles trailing behind them as they took their seats.

Seeking Sean's presence amidst the mounting tension, Lillian approached him, her footsteps purposeful. "Dinner is ready," she informed him, her words a bridge towards reconciliation. Yet, his bitter glare greeted her, a visual testament to the chasm that separated them. She turned away, allowing him the space to stew in his own troubled thoughts. She knew that provoking his temper would only fan the flames of their discord, an outcome she sought to avoid.

Around the table, they sat in a heavy silence. Unspoken grievances saturated the air. Sean brooded in the depths of his dark mood, deep furrows etched his face. Stella, her young spirit perceptive beyond her years, kept her gaze lowered. Two-year-old Mary, unaware of the simmering tension surrounding her, played with her food. The rugged handsomeness of her husband struck Lillian, despite the storm brewing beneath his exterior.

Lillian packed the remaining possessions of her family, each item a testament to the life they had built in this cherished house. She couldn't deny the truth that lived deep within her—she had no wish to uproot their existence.

The rumors, like tendrils of smoke, had crept into their lives, becoming the spark for their unwanted departure. They had already once escaped the tinderbox of idle whispers, seeking refuge out of town. The townsfolk held a limited understanding of Lillian and her abilities as a healer, and carried a fear that painted her actions with shades of dark magick. They danced with fire, ignorant of the repercussions that awaited them. It was the universal truth, an adage whispered through the ages, that one reaps what they sow.

Lillian petitioned the goddesses for ways to protect herself in the new home. She yearned for a life free from the clutches of those who sought to take advantage of her gifts, or worse, assign blame for their own misfortunes.

Countless were the souls she had healed, mending their wounds and easing their ailments. But there were those who expected miracles beyond the realm of her capabilities. Accusations swirled, fingers pointed, and whispers lingered in the air like a virulent breeze. A few dared to insinuate she was not of this world, a changeling draped in the cloak of a malevolent fairy.

The damning label of "witch" slipped from lips, ignorant of the grave consequences from such an accusation. Once that dreaded "w" word took flight, stories sprout like weeds, intertwining to form an impenetrable web of certainty, leaving no room for doubt in the minds of those who heard. It was a fate that befell many of her ancestors, a legacy she had inherited, and one she struggled to break free from.

Her mother and aunts accused her of paranoia. They dismissed her fears, believing her to exaggerate every threat that loomed on the horizon. But Lillian knew better. A mere sidelong glance from a stranger was enough to send a shiver along her spine, as if they were conspiring to orchestrate her downfall.

Fear was not the driving force behind her actions. It was an unyielding anger that coursed through her veins, fueling a deep-seated desire to halt those who dared to cross her and make them pay. But could she alter this aspect of herself? It seemed as futile as convincing a badger that not every shadow held a threat. Yet, as she lay there, thoughts of taming a lynx, of harnessing its ferocious spirit, crossed her mind—a symbol of her own determination to tame the raging beast in her.

As the night settled around them, the family laid down to rest. Sean turned away from Lillian without so much as a good night kiss, leaving her with a pang of hurt that resonated deep. She shifted to the other side, her tears hidden from their daughters nestled between them, determined not to expose her vulnerability.

Chapter Ten

The next morning arrived, casting its gentle light upon Lillian. She had many tasks to complete before they left for Carrick-on-Shannon. She prepared a modest breakfast of boiled potatoes and milk. Eager to finish the remaining packing, Lillian delved into the work.

Sean remained silent and sullen. Stella, ever helpful, assisted Lillian in loading the last of their belongings onto the cart. Meanwhile, Mary chased after their curious little kitten, who embarked on a small adventure as they prepared to leave.

When Lillian completed her tasks, she took a deep breath, casting a bittersweet gaze upon their beloved cottage. It was a sad farewell. But beneath the surface, excitement simmered within Lillian, anticipation of the fresh start that awaited them in a new place.

The journey that lay ahead would be arduous. Tethered to the wagon were their cherished dairy cow and a plump pig, which they had raised throughout the past year to cover their rent. Accompanied by these animals and their two young children, their progress would be slower. But Lillian welcomed this unhurried pace, for it allowed her ample time to gather herbs and plants along the way, taking advantage of the unfamiliar terrain they traversed.

Apprehension and excitement filled Lillian's heart as they embarked upon the road to Carrick-on-Shannon. They had squeezed their possessions into the horse-drawn cart, and the journey before them stretched out before them. Her determination burned bright, as she resolved to make the most of this challenging situation.

Regrettably, the new dwelling that awaited them in Carrick-on-Shannon proved to be smaller. Despite its size, the rent equaled that of their larger cottage. To make matters worse, the landlord only agreed to rent if Sean worked in his fields for less pay. This angered Sean because he couldn't work with sheep anymore.

The silence between Sean and Lillian made things worse. This move proved even harder than their earlier one, especially given Mary's tender age. The steady rhythm of Lillian's footsteps provided solace though, echoing upon the flat terrain and well-maintained road they tread on that first day of travel.

As they ventured forth, their future in the new location consumed Lillian's thoughts. No matter the challenges that lay ahead, she remained steadfast in her determination to make the best of their circumstances.

The night descended, shrouding their makeshift camp in an unsettling stillness. Weary from the day's travels, Lillian had drifted into a restless slumber, only to be awakened by a symphony of animal cries shattering the tranquility. The shrill squeal of their pig pierced the air, intertwined with the frantic neighs of their horse and the distressed moos of their cow.

Startled, Lillian jolted upright, her heart pounding in her chest. Something was amiss. Wide-eyed, she surveyed the darkness, striving to comprehend the chaos that unfolded around them. And there she beheld it.

A sleek and predatory wolf had crept up on their bound pig. The poor, determined creature fought, its terrified screams echoing through the night. The wolf was relentless, its claws scraping against the ground as it pounced upon its prey, powerful jaws sinking into the pig's vulnerable backside and neck.

Awoken by the commotion, Sean leaped to his feet, his voice a mixture of anger and fear as he sought to scare away the wolf. Yet, the predator paid no heed to his cries, consumed by its merciless pursuit. Despite Sean's valiant attempts, the wolf's might proved insurmountable. With a victorious growl, it dragged its stolen meal into the darkness, leaving behind a trail of loss and destruction.

Sean turned to Lillian, his anger palpable, frustration and resentment dripping from his words. "Damn it! If I hadn't sold my rifle to afford that blasted deposit on the new house, I might have taken that wolf. But no, thanks to you, Lillian, our pig is gone now. How much more of my life are you going to ruin?"

His sentiment hung in the air, icy and biting, causing Lillian's heart to ache. She struggled to comprehend the depth of blame he placed upon her shoulders. How had everything become her burden to bear? Lillian suppressed her weariness and overwhelming emotions, taking a steadying breath.

She overlooked Sean's bitter tirade and centered her attention on what she could manage. Lillian approached her frightened horse and cow, offering gentle words and soothing touches to calm their agitated spirits. As their trembling subsided, she directed her attention to her daughters, coaxing them back into peaceful slumber by singing a soft Irish lullaby that floated through the night.

Amidst turmoil and blame, Lillian clung to these fleeting moments of solace and connection. Her love and strength poured into the soothing melody that graced her lips. She refused to allow bitterness to consume her. Nor would she let the hardships they faced to rend their family apart. As her voice blended along the whispers of the night's wind, Lillian became a beacon of tranquility in the storm, striving to mend the shattered fragments of their fragile unity.

Over in Killarney
Many years ago,
Me Mother sang a song to me
In tones so sweet and low.
Just a simple little ditty,
In her good old Irish way,
And I'd give the world if she could sing
That song to me this day.

Too-ra-loo-ra-loo-ral, Too-ra-loo-ra-li,
Too-ra-loo-ra-loo-ral, hush now, don't you cry!
Too-ra-loo-ra-loo-ral, Too-ra-loo-ra-li,
Too-ra-loo-ra-loo-ral, that's an Irish lullaby.

Oft in dreams I wander
To that cot again,
I feel her arms a-huggin' me
As when she held me then.
And I hear her voice a-hummin'
To me, as in days of yore,
When she used to rock me fast asleep,
Outside the cabin door.

Too-ra-loo-ra-loo-ral, Too-ra-loo-ra-li,

Too-ra-loo-ra-loo-ral, hush now, don't you cry!
Too-ra-loo-ra-loo-ral, Too-ra-loo-ra-li,
Too-ra-loo-ra-loo-ral, that's an Irish lullaby.

The rest of the night weighed on Lillian's spirit after the wolf attack. Sean's accusatory words lingered in her mind, and the blame he placed on her shoulders became an unbearable burden. To avoid his presence, she fashioned a makeshift bed on the cart, wrapping herself in her coat. As sleep beckoned her, she contemplated ways to appease Sean, even considering slipping chamomile into his food or drink to calm his temperament. Yet, doubts crept in, raising questions about whether it was worth the effort to placate him. Should she prepare herself for a life without him? The thought unsettled her, but she knew she possessed the strength to support her daughters on her own.

The following day, the family continued their journey, but the rolling terrain proved to be a challenge. Lillian's feet ached, and her back protested from the constant walking along the winding roads.

Stella alternated between walking and riding in the wagon, keeping her sister, Mary, company. The toddler was fussy, unable to decide whether she wanted to walk or ride. Whenever her desires were not met, Mary acted out by throwing tantrums and causing difficulties. Lillian saw glimpses of her own fiery nature in her younger daughter.

Passing the picturesque Lough Allen, Lillian seized the opportunity to forage for herbs, having Stella by her side. She displayed a natural talent for making herbal teas, and Lillian took pride in her daughter's patience and determination.

As the second night descended upon them, they camped near the quiet village of Drumshanbo, Sean's hometown, nestled on the southern fringes of Lough Allen. Dinner consisted of fresh-caught fish roasted over crackling flames, accompanied by simple cattails.

A peaceful calmness filled their surroundings, luring everyone into a deep and uninterrupted sleep. Lillian and Sean rested, separated by their children and the emotional barriers erected by Lillian's acts of vengeance.

The next morning, they ventured into a foreign landscape. Lillian's earlier home had been within walking distance of Glenade Lough, nestled amidst a lush valley guarded by two towering mountains, their majestic cliffs reaching for the sky. Now, she found herself on a plain, where flax, wheat, and potatoes sprouted from the fertile earth.

At the broken gate of their new home, Lillian stood, taking in the sight. It was the pinnacle of poverty and the toughest conditions she had ever faced. The tiny one-room dwelling, constructed from meager sod and crowned by a thatched roof, boasted a primitive chimney fashioned from a humble wicker basket. She opened the feeble door, made of ill-fitting boards, which didn't seal out curious creatures seeking entry. The small window without glass was the only source of light in the dark interior and would be the source of winter winds.

Lillian's face twisted into a disapproving frown as she surveyed the scant furnishings—a table, a solitary stool, and an iron pot resting in the hearth.

To meet their new obligations required Lillian to sell her herbal remedies and Sean to use his leather crafting skills, while also working in the landlord's fields. Losing their pig only intensified the challenges they faced.

Within Lillian's heart, a profound realization took hold and blossomed. The austere house and the grueling existence it entailed were her penance, a cruel retribution for past misdeeds. She needed to make amends.

Being a young mother and selling her herbal remedies in town proved to be a tough challenge for Lillian during the first few months. In Carrick-on-Shannon, she couldn't afford a booth like she had in Manorhamilton, so she carried a basket in the crook of one arm while holding Mary's hand. Stella helped by taking care of the money.

One evening, while Lillian prepared soup for her family, there was a sudden knock on her door. It startled her because nobody had knocked since they moved there. Lillian's heart raced as she hurried to answer it, fearing it might be bad news about Sean working in the fields. She tried to push away her fear of the worst outcome. Standing outside was a pregnant woman whom Lillian had seen in a nearby field.

"Can I help you?" Lillian asked.

The woman placed a hand on her belly. "My sister said you're a healer. My son is sick."

"Yes, I am a healer. Please come in. Would you like some tea?" Lillian replied, holding the door open. She was worried about the condition of her small house, with only a few chairs and a table. It differed from their earlier home, and she felt uncomfortable living in the drafty sod house.

"No," the woman responded, perching on the edge of a chair, looking ready to leave at any moment.

"I'm Lillian," she introduced herself, sitting on a stool by the fire.

"I'm Nan," the pregnant woman replied.

Lillian asked. "What ails your son?"

Nan rubbed her face before answering, "His throat hurts, he has a fever, and he's sleeping a lot. I can't get him to eat."

"I have a tonic that might help. Give it to him in the morning and evening," Lillian said, rising and opening a bag under her bed. She took out a bottle, hesitating about charging Nan since she had saved her a trip to town. "Since you're a neighbor, I'll only ask for a ten pence deposit for the bottle."

Nan took the bottle and put it in her apron pocket after giving Lillian the money. "Thank you."

"Please let me know how he's doing in a few days. If this doesn't work, I have another one. There are two similar sicknesses that need different herbs," Lillian said, showing her to the door, hoping Sean would come home after Nan left. She wanted to have dinner ready for him, and he had lost interest in her herbal business since they moved. Lillian decided not to put the deposit in the rent jar because she didn't want to take money out once it was in there.

This was the business Lillian wanted. If customers came to her, she wouldn't have to take her children to town all the time. But she still had to cook, clean, tend to the garden, and make her daily trips. It was hard work, and if she could find a simpler way to make money, she would do it.

Three days later, Lillian heard the same rapid knock on her door. She hurried to open it and found Nan standing there, this time smiling. "Come in."

"I just wanted to tell you he's much better and helping me in the garden again. Here's the bottle," Nan said, tapping her chest.

"Come in," Lillian said, holding the door open. Nan stepped inside, hesitating before crossing the threshold. Lillian sensed her unease but didn't push her. She walked over to a spot above the hearth to get Nan's deposit.

"Here's your deposit," Lillian said, turning back to Nan. "I'm glad your son is better. Are you sure you don't have a moment? I can do a tarot reading for you. No charge. We're neighbors."

Nan looked at the door and then through the window opening. After a moment, she shrugged. "If it won't take long. I have to be back before my husband. He doesn't know I'm gone."

Lillian smiled, happy to use her tarot cards. She took them out from a bag under her bed and brought them to the table. "A quick spread then. Past, present, and future."

As Lillian turned over the card for the future, her heart sank. It showed the image of death, but she didn't want to tell a pregnant woman something bad. It was hard to find the right words to explain the different meanings of the card.

"You don't have to say anything. I know what that card means. Someone close to me will die," Nan said, her eyes stopping at something on the wall. Tears welled up in her eyes.

Lillian gathered the cards, her chest tightening. She noticed Nan staring at Sean's cross. "Maybe it means something else, like an end to something, like the nice weather we've been having."

Nan stood, a tear falling onto the table. "It doesn't mean that. I have to go." She rushed out the door, letting it slam shut.

Lillian stood for a moment, taking deep breaths to calm herself, biting her lip. A fly drank from Nan's tear, and Lillian caught it. She walked over to the door, opened it, and put the fly in the web made by an orb weaver spider in the corner of the door frame. She pushed the fly onto the web until it stuck, then watched as the spider spun a thread around the struggling insect to hide it in a cocoon for a tasty meal later.

The circle of life fascinated Lillian. It was sad to be a fly, everyone wanting to end you, even horses tired of flies biting them all day. People didn't like spiders, but they controlled the population of annoying bugs. Lillian let the spiders be. She would rather be a friend to the spider and help it find food.

Chapter Eleven

Lillian and Stella were on their hands and knees in the garden, battling stubborn weeds as the scorching sun beat down on them. Beads of sweat rolled down their foreheads, but Lillian didn't mind. The work kept her grounded, connected to the earth. Little Mary, oblivious to the world around her, dangled earthworms for her kitten nearby.

A man's panicked voice shattered the peacefulness of the garden. "Healer! Healer! I need your help!" Lillian looked up to see a stranger rushing towards her, skin bunched around his eyes.

"What do you need a healer for?" Lillian asked, rising to her feet and dusting off her apron. She reached for her herbal bag, ready to offer her help.

"It's my wife," the man gasped, his voice trembling. "Her labor is going wrong. Hurry!" He waved his hand, signaling her to follow him as he headed for the gate.

Lillian's heart raced, the urgency in the man's voice sending a jolt of tension through her. She ushered her children into the house. "Stella, I need you to take care of your sister until your father or I come home. Don't answer the door for anyone." Her voice carried a sense of urgency and importance as she spoke.

Leaving her children behind, Lillian followed the desperate man to his home. She feared for what she might find. What if the situation was dire? What if the mother and baby were in danger? She dreaded the challenges of midwifery, knowing the risks involved.

The man hurried into the room where his wife lay, writhing in pain. Lillian approached the bed, trying to keep a calm demeanor. "May I?" she asked, seeking permission to examine the woman.

Nan nodded, her face contorted with agony. Lillian placed her ear on Nan's belly, listening for the reassuring sound of a heartbeat. But she heard nothing. She tried different spots, hoping for a different outcome, but the room remained silent. The baby had passed away.

Lillian's heart sank, but she knew she couldn't let Nan know the devastating news, especially after the earlier encounter with the death card. Now, her focus shifted to saving Nan's life, fighting against the gripping despair that threatened to consume her.

Lillian sprang into action, relying on her experience and skills to navigate the delicate process of delivering the baby. Despite her best efforts, when the moment came, the baby lay lifeless in her hands.

Overwhelmed by grief, the husband's anger erupted. "This is your fault!" he shouted, his voice full of accusation. "She told me about your cursed cards and what they said. You brought this misfortune upon us!"

The man's rage intensified, his fists clenching and unclenching by his sides. In a fit of fury, he dashed to the hearth, snatched a rifle, and aimed it at Lillian. His eyes bulged, teeth bared.

Fear gripped Lillian's heart as she backed away, her hands raised in a desperate plea for mercy. "Please, don't shoot! I saved your wife's life," she pleaded, her voice trembling. The threat of imminent danger was palpable, her heart pounding within her chest. In a rush of adrenaline, she stumbled towards the door and fled from the house, running as fast as her feet would carry her until she reached the sanctuary of her own home.

As Lillian swung open the door, a wave of relief washed over her at the peaceful sight of Stella peeling potatoes and Mary snoring. "Oh, my dear children. I missed you," she murmured, her voice attempting to mask the turmoil within. Though she appeared composed, an underlying tremor of fear lingered within her. She had escaped a life-threatening situation, all because of the superstitious beliefs of a grieving husband.

The following day, Sunday, was a peaceful day of rest and relaxation for the family. They spent part of it in their yard, tending to their garden and taking care of their cow, enjoying the sunshine and gentle breeze. Lillian wished they had more days like this, where she forgot all her troubles and enjoyed her family.

Nan's husband burst through the gate, his face twisted in anger. He stormed towards Sean, his voice booming, "She should pay!"

Sean rubbed his chin and asked, "What ken I do for you?"

Leaning into Sean chest to chest, the man said, "Don't you know? Your wife cursed mine, killing our baby!" He sneered, "And she calls herself a healer."

Sean had the size and strength to take down the man, but violence would not be his answer. Instead, Sean turned to glare at her. Lillian's stomach roiled, and a chill washed over her.

The accusations hung heavy in the air, causing Lillian's heart to race. The man's grief overwhelmed him, but rage burned in his eyes. Lillian wished she had told Sean about the incident, but she never thought the man would be hellbent on causing trouble. "The child was stillborn. I saved Nan's life. That's all I'm able to do. You pointed a rifle at me." Lillian clutched her chest, remembering the barrel pointing at her. "And you didn't pay me for my services."

Stella cowered from the scene, whimpering.

Sean leaned into the man. "You heard her. She saved your wife's life. That should pay for it. Leave! You're upsetting my children."

Before the man stormed out the gate, he raised a fist.

Lillian ushered the girls into the safety of their home, hoping that Sean would stay outside for a while. When he didn't come in, she pulled out her altar, lighting two candles. She sent Ean carrying two small envelopes to retrieve items from the man's property.

When Ean returned, she poured the milk from one envelope into a small glass jar, followed by the dirt from the other envelope. She whispered a spell over the jar, words of power and intent.

By the powers of the earth and sky,
I cast this spell to nullify,
The milk and dirt within this jar,
And make them have no charge.
May the milk come out putrid,
From the cow's udders polluted,
May the fields from which this dirt came,
Be cursed with ruin and never the same.
As I light this flame, let it burn and
Use magick and power to overturn
All the positive, all the fortune,

Let this spell bring them ruin.
So mote it be!

A spark turned into a flame. As the flames danced, she released a deep, satisfying sigh, knowing justice had been served.

She cleansed the altar and slid it under her bed, mouth pinched, eyes half closed. Sean's cross hung in every home they lived, but her practice had to remain hidden, out-of-sight. Her beliefs flew in the face of Sean's religion and the religion of almost everyone in the country.

Lillian set about to make fresh bread, Sean's favorite, for dinner. Food worked to subside any of her husband's anger, most of the time. She buried her anger deep inside her, to fester and fuel her dark side.

Through gaining all the powers of air, fire, water, and earth it made her the rarest of witches. But she had to keep that hidden. What would other witches feel about her powers? She feared a jealous witch more than anything. Since witches kept hushed about their reality, anyone she met might be one. Better not to trust anyone, just in case. Any confrontation could be deadly. Were there any other witches like her? Would she ever get an answer to that? They would hide their powers like her for their safety. The world was a cruel place for a witch.

Lillian sighed. She wasn't supposed to do any vengeful things or evil spells on anyone in this new location. How was supposed to sit by and let this man defame, slander, and threaten her? She saved his wife's life, and she received no thanks for her efforts. They didn't even compensate her, so it came across to her as being cheated as well. But she feared going to the magistrate about that because the death of the infant would be front and center and might go against her. Best to keep her head low and watch the dust settle around her pushed-down fury.

Chapter Twelve

With the basket of her most popular remedies nestled in the crook of her arm, Lillian made her way along the dirt lane towards town. The teas had proven to be the most sought-after remedies, their lighter weight and ease of transport making them a customer favorite compared to the potent brews that required glass bottles. Walking alongside her, Stella carried a satchel containing a few coins jingling inside, while Mary skipped by Lillian's side, their hands intertwined.

As she passed her neighbor's empty house, it reminded Lillian of the fragility of life and how quick everything could change. Death and loss were familiar companions to her after many years of practicing the healing arts. In the face of the vacant home, a faint smile tugged at the corners of her lips. *No one will intimidate me.*

The heart of the town unfolded before them as they reached the bustling square adorned with vibrant booths showcasing various goods. Food, flowers, jewelry, and fabric clamored for attention, enticing nearby shoppers.

The exorbitant fee demanded by Mr. St. George, the wealthy marketplace owner, in Carrick-on-Shannon, dissuaded her from setting up a booth here. She refused to be exploited to support his lavish lifestyle.

Instead, Lillian edged her way through the crowd, proclaiming her remedies for all to hear. "Remedies for fevers, chills, and sleeplessness!" Her voice soared above the market's din, drawing potential customers to her side.

But, sales were sluggish on this day. Lillian sensed tension in the air, the way people averted their gaze. It wasn't mere imagination. A woman stepped forward, her face twisted. "They left because of you! My sister is gone." She placed her finger on Lillian's chest, making her back away. "You killed her baby and brought a curse upon their land. You are to blame for it all!" Venom dripped from the woman's accusations, and her companions echoed her words.

Lillian's heart raced as she grasped Mary's hand. They ran down a nearby street, escaping the square and the wrath of the enraged women. Once they were distant, Stella burst into tears, while Mary looked at Lillian, eyes wide. "Why were we running? You run too fast."

"I'm sorry, my dear. Stella, please don't cry. Everything will be fine. That woman had a terrible day, and she took her frustrations out on me." Even as Lillian attempted to reassure them, she knew the situation was far more dire than it appeared. How many people knew about her neighbor's misfortunes? How many pinned the blame on her? If these rumors spread, they could destroy her livelihood, leaving her and Sean unable to pay rent or buy food.

Determined to alter the course of events, Lillian guided the children back to the square. She knew that her remedy, meant to ease fevers, possessed the potential to evoke them when given the right incantations. Magick was a fickle force, capable of both good and evil. Like cured like, but like could also condemn like. Moving through the crowd, she sprinkled her remedy, uttering a spell under her breath.

With every footstep, this spell does spread,
A feverish illness, a sickness widespread.
From soul to soul, the magick leaps,
A footstep's touch, a fever it keeps.
So mote it be!

As Lillian traversed the marketplace, her magpie familiar swooped and perched on various vendor booths and carts. It was a subtle gesture, but she understood people's superstitions. The Church of Ireland had failed to squash the deep-rooted beliefs of the Irish people, no matter how hard they tried. The bird's presence would stir concerns of ill fortune, diverting attention from the brewing rumors of witchcraft and curses.

As the day drew to a close, Lillian guided her children back home, her mind already engrossed in the tasks that lay ahead. Tomorrow, she would carry only one remedy, but in copious amounts.

Lillian awoke early, plans for the day buzzing in her mind. The latest cure for the fever that would have afflicted the town since yesterday overfilled her basket. Each sachet promised relief from the relentless fever she had addressed the day before.

Mary's mood was already turning sour, but Lillian sprung into action. She pressed her thumb against the child's forehead and chanted a spell to keep her temper in check.

Let her anger and frustration cease,
And fill her heart with love and peace,
May she find joy in every breath,
And be content with all that's left.
So mote it be!

Pressing forward toward the square, the burden of the laden basket and the bustling crowd weighed on them. Lillian had Stella by her side, a small satchel of money slung over the girl's shoulder. She had crafted a protective amulet for her, one that would deter any potential thieves or attackers. A potent curse awaited those foolish enough to lay a hand on her child, rendering them helpless and writhing on the ground.

When they made it to the square, a throng of people, all clamoring for Lillian's remedies, swallowed them. Some were ailing themselves, while others sought aid for their loved ones. Stella's hands were busy collecting each sale and placing them in the satchel.

As she closed each deal, a surge of adrenaline fueled her excitement for the profits that lay ahead. By midday, Lillian had sold out of her remedies, promising to return the following day.

On the walk home, they sang and laughed, their voices carrying in the countryside. Lillian held her head high, inhaling to relish the sweet satisfaction of her achievements. Without a second thought, she passed by her old neighbor's house, while brainstorming new ways to profit from other ailments to exploit for profit. Carrick-on-Shannon proved to be fertile ground for her business, and she would seize every opportunity it presented.

The archbishop's ornate carriage halted in front of the city hall. He stepped out, preoccupied with the Bishop's complaints about a cursed deceased infant and his unyielding conviction that dangerous forces were at play. It had reached a fervent pitch, calling for immediate action.

Upon entering the magistrate's outer office, the archbishop said in a confident and powerful voice that left no room for hesitation, "I must see the magistrate immediately."

The meek assistant behind the desk recoiled from the archbishop's brusqueness. "You are early for his office hours, sir," he stuttered.

"I am never early. Fetch him at once," the archbishop retorted, his impatience swelling by the second. Gatekeepers were a vexation, and he possessed no tolerance for their hindrances. They could pen their grievances and send them to him, but their complaints would serve only as tinder for his righteous fire. That is what prayer was for.

Nudging the door ajar, the assistant announced the archbishop's arrival. The magistrate's response remained inaudible, but now the archbishop knew he was present. He would not leave without speaking to him. His time held immense value, and he had no intention of returning.

"You may enter," the assistant stammered, pushing the door open.

The towering archbishop entered the room. He ducked at the doorway to avoid dislodging his biretta while his black and purple cassock billowing around him like a formidable sail. Settling into a seat across from the magistrate, he leaned forward, locking his gaze onto the man's face.

When the magistrate steepled his hands, putting on an air of importance, the archbishop dismissed the notion. No one held greater significance than the Church, not even the King.

"What can I do for His Excellency today?" the magistrate asked, his smug smile doing little, as actions, not false smiles, determined one's path to heaven.

"We face a grave issue that demands immediate attention," the archbishop said, his tone conveying the weight of the matter. "A pious family has fallen victim to a curse. Their newborn arrived breathless, their fields lie barren, and their cow yields sour milk. Reduced to destitution, they endure the anguish of public shame. A neighbor, a self-proclaimed healer, engaged in tarot card readings and inflicted this curse upon the unfortunate woman. You must take action."

The archbishop hoped the magistrate grasped the urgency of the situation. With the Bishop involved, swift measures were crucial; failure to do so could spell trouble for the magistrate and himself.

"I require more information. Who is this woman responsible for the curse?" the magistrate asked.

A sigh escaped the archbishop, weary of having to reiterate himself. "The woman is a neighbor—her whereabouts should be apparent. She presents herself as a healer. I have witnessed her parading two children around town, peddling supposed remedies from a basket. Of course, she doesn't attend any of the local churches."

The magistrate leaned forward, placing his hands flat on the desk. "I shall begin an immediate investigation. If I find evidence, I shall take the woman into custody."

The archbishop rose, his immediate mission accomplished. He vowed to keep a watchful eye on things to ensure that the magistrate fulfilled his duties. The Bishop would not forget. "I commend you recognizing of the gravity of this matter. We cannot permit evil to flourish. Once it takes root, removal becomes a monumental task."

The archbishop's biretta avoided snagging on the door frame as he ducked through the doorway. With a final disdainful glance at the meek assistant, he raised his hand, extending two fingers in a blessing. He strode out of the magistrate's outer office surrounded in ethereal haughtiness and into the embrace of the warm sunshine.

Down the steps of the city hall, the archbishop contemplated the perils of tarot cards. They were instruments used by the devil to ensnare vulnerable souls, much like the self-proclaimed healer who had wrought havoc upon the devout family. Perhaps he should advocate a ban on these treacherous implements, putting an end to such disturbances within the district once and for all.

Chapter Thirteen

As Lillian and Stella tended to the garden, Lillian enjoyed the sun's warmth on her skin and was surrounded by the intoxicating scent of blooming flowers and herbs. Mary frolicked with the cat, a small wicker basket perched nearby. Ean's sharp warning call, his staccato 'chac-chac-chac-chac,' shattered the tranquility, jolting Lillian's senses. She recognized the significance of that sound all too well.

The rhythmic thud of hooves reached her ears. Moments later, an older man clad in resplendent attire atop a horse arrived, intruding upon the serenity of their home. Stepping out of the garden, Lillian extended her hand, signaling for Stella to stay where she was. She stood tall, preparing herself for whatever this man sought.

"Are you Lillian Maguire?" he inquired, dismounting and tethering his horse to a nearby post.

Lillian nodded, her heart racing faster with each passing moment. "I am. What brings you here?"

The man introduced himself as Patrick Reynolds, the magistrate in Carrick-on-Shannon. Lillian's muscles tensed, her mind raced. What could a magistrate want with her? A magistrate was the last person she wanted to see.

"I have some questions for you," Patrick said, his voice aloof. "Is there somewhere we can sit? My knees are troublesome."

Lillian gestured towards the house for him to follow. "Of course. Come inside." She ushered Mary and Stella indoors, holding the door open for him. "Would you like some tea?"

"Please." Patrick settled at the table, where Stella pulled out a chair for him. "Thank you, my dear. You are quite sweet."

Stella nodded and hurried over to join Mary in play.

Flushed with embarrassment, Lillian watched as he surveyed their humble sod house. Preparing a blend of chamomile, willow bark, and honey—a concoction to soothe him and ease his knee discomfort—she set the cup of tea before him, then took a seat across the table, studying him. "What questions do you have for me?" she asked, her voice striving to keep a steady composure. She couldn't fathom what he could ask, unless her neighbor had accused her of causing the baby's demise before fleeing town. But that had been weeks ago.

"You're a healer?" Patrick inquired, his gaze penetrating hers.

Lillian nodded. "Yes, I have been for a considerable time."

"Did you attend to your neighbor as a midwife?" he pressed further.

"I did. And before you jump to any conclusions, the baby had no heartbeat before birth. At that point, I sought only to save the mother's life. There was no use in having two lives lost."

"The father alleges you cursed his wife, resulting in the baby's death. What interactions did you have with the mother prior to the birth?"

Lillian released a weary sigh, the weight of the accusations bearing down upon her. "I provided a remedy for her son, and he recovered," she replied, omitting the fact that she had also conducted a card reading for the woman. She knew better than to divulge anything that could further incriminate her.

"Did you engage in tarot card readings?"

"No. She mentioned not having the time."

"I see. Well, the Church disapproves of tarot cards. They consider it blasphemy."

Lillian raised an eyebrow. "So I've heard. Are you also here representing the Church? They are against folk remedies, content to let their people perish."

"I must request that you cease performing any midwifery duties here. It is for your own safety. I have no further inquiries and shall take my leave," Patrick declared, rising from his seat. "I hope I'll not need to cross paths with you again. Thank you for the tea. It was quite good."

Relief washed over Lillian as he departed, discarding the remnants of his tea outside the front door. Yet, deep within her, she sensed that this was far from the end. The Church maintained a watchful eye, an ever-present listener to the whispers of the community.

"Are you in trouble?" Stella asked.

"No, my dear. He was curious," Lillian reassured them, attempting to allay their fears.

Mary chimed in, "He's out of his mind!"

Lillian chuckled. "No, he's not out of his mind. You've heard your Da say that."

She guided the girls back outside to resume their chores, her mind a whirlwind of anxious thoughts, a symphony of unease orchestrating a frenzy within. As much as she tried, she could not find respite or clarity amidst the overwhelming tide of apprehension.

As Sean approached his home, the ache in his back from a long day of labor in the fields intensified. The yearning for relief from Lillian's poultice overwhelmed him.

He spotted a well-equipped horse in the yard. Confusion gripped him. Who could be with Lillian? As he reached for the rope serving as the doorknob, a man's voice emanated from inside. Panic surged through his chest, and he approached the window, attempting to eavesdrop. His mind conjured the worst-case scenario—was Lillian involved with a wealthy man from town? He leaned in closer, his heart racing, hoping to catch snippets of their conversation.

Sean was relieved to find out that his worst fears did not come true. Instead, the magistrate questioned her, and disappointment washed over him. Lillian had reverted to her earlier behavior, and Sean reproached himself for believing she had changed.

When the man mentioned his departure, Sean rushed to the shed, pretending to be engrossed in a task.

The well-dressed man exited the house and made his way toward his horse.

Emerging from the shed, Sean inquired, "Is everything alright?"

Patrick startled. "Yes, all is well," he replied, mounting his horse and departing through the gate. Sean noticed his evasiveness, leaving him wondering what had transpired within the house.

Memories of the past flooded back, and the same apprehensions crept up again. Next, the impending rumors would soon spread, branding Lillian as a witch. Sean had witnessed it all before—the accusations, suspicion, and fear. Every time he implored her to cease her actions, she would dismiss the claims, attributing them to jealousy towards her abilities. What if the townspeople were right and Lillian possessed witch-like powers? What would that make him and his daughters?

As Sean pondered his past decisions, doubts enveloped his mind. Had Lillian enchanted him?

The family left behind their home in Manorhamilton to start a new life far away from the rumors. He made a vow that he wouldn't move again. No more fresh starts. They never got ahead.

This time, they settled in a smaller house on a smaller plot of land. The sense of failing as a father overwhelmed him. Unease clutched at him, especially about his youngest daughter. Everything seemed amiss. He yearned to return to his own family—the ones who had warned him that marrying Lillian was a mistake.

The uncertainty and regret overwhelmed him as he entered the house and began packing his scant belongings into a fabric bag. It was a disheartening sight—a man leaving his home with little more than the clothes on his back. Sean reached a breaking point. Change was necessary, and it had to happen now.

Lillian grabbed his arm, questioning, "What are you doing? Where are you going?"

Sean pulled away, his voice resolute. "I'm leaving. I told you I wouldn't go through this again."

Lillian blocked the doorway, and Stella ran to embrace him.

"Don't go, Da!" Stella pleaded.

It pained him to hear those words, but it wasn't enough to dissuade him any longer. Lillian wrapped her arms around him. "Please, please don't leave me and the girls. Stay, at least for the girls.

He asked that I refrain from practicing midwifery. I explained that nothing untoward occurred, that the child had already passed before my arrival. I won't pursue midwifery anymore. There's nothing to worry about. Please stay. I love you."

"I love you too, Da," Stella said through her sobs, still clinging to his leg.

Sean looked at Stella, tears streaming down her face, and his heart broke. "The other family didn't depart because of that. Their cow produced sour milk, their fields turned barren." His determination wavered, melting away like the last remnants of winter snow on a spring day. "Fine. I'll stay for Stella. But understand, it won't take much for me to leave soon."

"I'm sure the rumors will cease in time. Once the excitement dies, they'll fade away," Lillian reassured him. He knew this ordeal was taking a toll on her. She couldn't control her nature. But he couldn't control his own misgivings. The constant attention their family attracted, because of Lillian's unexplainable deeds or their allegations, unsettled him. If she possessed witch-like powers, it contradicted everything he had learned in church and accepted as truth throughout his life. It tore him apart, torn between his deep love for her and the uncertainty of that love being genuine. If she were indeed a witch. The conflict tormented him, inflicting an ache in his heart and soul.

Lillian took his bag and stowed away his belongings while he observed. She handled them with tender care, mesmerizing him. He shook his head, wondering if she bewitched him once more, her beautiful black hair cascading over her shoulder, her fair skin, and her green eyes. Captivating. Was it all witchcraft, and she ensnared him in her spell?

As Lillian finished unpacking, she turned to him, eyes pleading. "Please, Sean. Let's not let this tear us apart. Together, we can overcome it."

Sean stared into her eyes, searching for any hint of deceit. He found none. Still, the unease lingered. He sighed. "For now, I'll stay. But if anything happens again, I'm gone. Do you understand?"

Lillian nodded, relief washing over her face. "I do. I'll do anything to make things right. For you and the girls."

Sean turned to Stella, who still clung to his leg. He kneeled to embrace her. "I'm not going anywhere, sweetheart. I'll be here for you."

Stella smiled through her tears, and Sean felt a pang of guilt. He didn't want to hurt his family, but he also couldn't ignore the doubts that persisted in his mind.

As they settled into bed that night, a sense of unease persisted within Sean. He questioned whether he had made the right choice in staying. But as Lillian nestled against him, her warmth enveloping him, he pushed those thoughts aside. For now, he resolved to make things work. Yet, if circumstances took a turn for the worse, he knew what he needed to do.

Chapter Fourteen

LILLIAN MEANDERED THROUGH THE bustling town square, remedies overflowing, her woven basket swaying at her side. Each time she visited, a peculiar old woman never failed to appear. Even though she had purchased nothing, her cheeks were rosy, and she was in better health than most of the people living in the town. Lillian looked forward to their talks; the woman was a veritable treasure trove of information about the area and its people.

Today, the old woman stood out even more than usual. A vibrant blue scarf encased her head, its loose ends fluttering in the breeze and contrasting against the bountiful waves of gray hair that spilled out from beneath it. As she approached, the old woman's eyes twinkled, and she had a knowing smile. "Have you heard of Irish Lady's Tresses?" she asked, a melodic lilt in her voice.

Lillian paused in her task of organizing her stock, interest piqued. "Yes. Very rare."

"I saw some when I visited a cousin," the old woman said, her gaze distant, as if she relived the memory. "We strolled to the stream and there they were. Seven. A lucky number."

While trying to suppress her excitement, Lillian asked, "Where is this stream?"

The old woman's eyes narrowed, and her lips pursed as if she weighed a heavy decision. "I shouldn't tell you. They are rare and the most exquisite plant."

Lillian released Mary's hand and crossed her fingers behind her back, her heart pounding in her chest. "I won't disturb them. I promise"

The old woman studied Lillian for a moment, her eyes softening. "Well then. You go down the road to Leitrim City. Not far. It's on the right past the large wheat field." Her crooked index finger rose, pointing at Lillian's chest, causing her to lean back. "You be sure not to harm those orchids."

The old woman turned away, vanishing into the throngs of shoppers like a specter, leaving Lillian to ponder the mysterious orchids and the rare healing they give. A life extension afforded by the rich.

Lillian's basket of remedies felt insignificant compared to the knowledge that the woman held. She couldn't shake off the notion that there was something more to this encounter than just a chance meeting.

As she continued her rounds, Lillian found herself lost in thought, her mind wandering to the Irish Lady's Tresses. She had learned of the plant before, but had never seen it in person. It bloomed in wet years, but still a rare sight. Her mother found one plant when Lillian was young and charged so much, they bought their cow and had a barn built to house it.

Lillian lived off the road the old woman spoke of. The wheat field was past their landlord's fields on a rolling hill that broke off into a crevice of trees, signaling a stream or spring. She took the children, followed the old woman's directions, and scanned the stream for a while. And then she saw them. Seven stalks in shallow water. Spikes of creamy white flowers twisting in a small spiral atop an erect, pale green stem. The beauty created a sense of awe to wash over her.

Stella and Mary both said, "Ahh. Can we pick them?"

Lillian shook her head. She approached the orchids, mindful of the old woman's warning, but she didn't collect them yet. For them to be powerful medicine, they had to be picked on a full moon.

On the night of the first full moon, a week later, Lillian emerged from her humble sod home. In order not to disturb Sean, she had foregone dressing and instead wore her flowing white chemise. The temperature was just right, neither too chilly nor too warm. Her shift billowed around her as she hastened towards the nearby stream. The full moon illuminated the surroundings with its radiant glow, casting a pale light that formed a path for Lillian to follow.

Under the moon's enchanting beams, the flowers along the stream emitted an ethereal luminescence, beckoning her to draw nearer. Kneeling beside the vibrant orchids, Lillian placed her sachet beside her and extracted a small knife. With practiced precision, she uprooted each plant, slicing a part of the root while ensuring that enough remained for future growth. She had to work quick, knowing that any misstep could cause the loss of these precious plants. The harvested root fragments found their place within her satchel, a valuable bounty.

As Lillian continued her task, a rustling sound startled her. She cleansed her knife in the stream and directed her gaze to the top of the steep embankment, where the silhouette of a man carrying a rifle came into view.

The man said, his voice booming, "What are you doing on my land in your nightgown in the middle of the night?"

Lillian clutched her satchel, though it didn't conceal enough of her form. Her heart raced, and she endeavored to keep her composure. "I am in search of a specific healing flower, and this was the only place I found it. I was unaware that this land belonged to someone. My apologies. I will take my leave."

The man bellowed, "You better leave. My hounds won't cease until you're gone. I need some peace."

Gathering her belongings, Lillian watched as Ean, ever loyal, swooped down, startling the farmer, who turned and fled. She retraced her steps along the stream, relieved to have escaped unscathed. Ean, however, had not reappeared.

Upon reaching her gate, Lillian dreaded its creaking sound waking Sean, and thus she climbed over the short stone wall. She entered the house, her fear of the farmer's potential pursuit lingering in her thoughts. As she settled into bed, she heard a faint tapping sound. A sigh of relief eluded her lips, knowing that Ean had returned, ready to protect her. She vowed to exercise greater caution in the future. With the valuable roots in her possession, she had the means to provide for her family once she found a buyer willing to appreciate their worth.

Lillian's sales had soared ever since Lillian's cursed walk around the town square. People clamored for her cures and potions, willing to pay whatever she asked. She didn't even have to spend much time in town anymore, as she sold out, no matter how full she stuffed her basket. The townspeople awaited her arrival, hoping to cure themselves or their loved ones at home.

As Lillian made her way back home, chin held high, shoulders back. The money she earned, she deposited into the rent jar, ensuring that they had a roof over their heads.

A few days before the rent was due, Lillian entered the house carrying carrots. Sean counted the money from the jar. "There is extra that I'm putting away for emergencies", he said.

Lillian nodded as she cut carrots for a stew. "But we need a chest," she said, her voice trailing. "This house has almost no furniture, and we had to leave much behind."

Sean shook his head. "No. We can get one later. We need money put aside for emergencies."

Lillian furrowed her brow, frustration bubbling inside her. Since most of that money was what she had earned, she should have a say. But she knew that if she said anything, it would bruise Sean's ego. Instead, she would make more money and buy the chest, anyway. After all, she still had the Irish Lady's Tresses roots.

That evening, Lillian spent hours making creams for a contagious rash. Tomorrow she would spread the rash as she sold her teas for the latest fever. Not to her direct customers, of course, but to others around her. She had no difficulty in spreading the contagion in the crowds of the marketplace.

While she worked, Lillian couldn't shake the nagging feeling that it might be the wrong thing to do. Her reasoning was that since no one was being killed or maimed, there was no harm. She needed to spread the new malady, which was the way of the system. The wealthy had reached their success by taking advantage of other people, and that was her plan.

Lillian walked into town accompanied by her girls, their steps light and quick. She enjoyed these walks. The girls chatted about their favorite flowers and what pie they'd make for supper. She forgot about her troubles when she was with them. As they passed by the familiar farms, she spotted the interesting old woman she saw every day.

Lillian gave her a warm smile. "Good morning. How are you this beautiful morning?"

The old woman didn't salute her magpie, only winked. "Good. And yourself and your two precious girls?"

Lillian stopped when she reached the woman. "Good. Do you want to try a tea to help you sleep? No cost."

The old woman smiled, wrinkles wrinkling upon wrinkles. "I have no need. But I need to warn you before you reach the market of a rumor started by my cousin's husband."

Lillian's heart sank. Of course, there would be a rumor; there've been rumors since she was born. Her grandmother had warned that she would be a danger to all who crossed her path, and to those who crossed her. "What fantasy have they cooked up?"

"He says he found you by his creek bed dancing in the nude with the devil on a clear full moon night. And when he shot at you, you vanished." She opened one eye more than the other, a slight tilt to her head. "What say you?"

Lillian gritted her teeth. She had been careless that night. "That is a quite a fantastical tale. He must have a big imagination."

"There's always some truth to a tall tale," the old woman said, her eyes twinkling.

"I visited that flower you told me about. I thought it would be more remarkable in the moonlight. And it was. I can tell you that. He came and told me to leave, and I did. The end. Nothing more." Lillian shifted the basket on her arm to a more comfortable position. The anger tightened all the muscles in her body. "Thank you for the warning. You are a genuine friend."

In one swift action, the elderly woman raised her lower lip and eyebrows, making them appear connected. "You seem a sincere person to me, and that's important. Stay safe, young lady. You have a family to think about. I must be going. Standing around won't keep me young." The woman continued on her way.

Lillian stood there, staring after the old woman. Was she a loyal friend or an enemy acting like a friend? Lillian kept everyone at arm's length, to be sure. She was not afraid of rumors, but this one could be dangerous. She had plenty of chores awaiting her at home. Not being one to back off from a challenge, she plowed ahead to face the rumor.

As they continued to town, Lillian talked about all the things they would buy with the extra money she made to distract her from the disturbing conversation.

Lillian shouted when she spied a neighbor, "Good morning, Siobhan." The neighbor glared at her and raced to the other side of the lane. Lillian asked, "What's wrong?" The neighbor didn't answer, but recited the Lord's prayer.

In town, several people gave her a wide berth and those who Lillian knew ignored her attempts to talk to her. As she passed by a group of women gathered around a well, their hushed whispers stopped as she approached. Lillian could sense their eyes on her, scrutinizing her every move. She fought the urge to turn and run, instead kept her head high and her pace steady. Until she ran into Ellen.

"If I had known you were the devil's servant, I would never had spoken to you. Now I have to go to confession and repent." Ellen's words were a slap in the face. Lillian's cheeks flushed. How could they believe such lies?

She opened her mouth to defend herself, but before she could utter a word, an egg struck her apron. Lillian recoiled, disgusted and furious. The sticky yolk dripped. She wanted to scream at the top of her lungs, but she knew it wouldn't change anything.

Lillian spat. "That story is not true. I don't dance with the devil."

Lillian wiped her hands on a vendor's booth curtain, trying to rid herself of the slimy egg. The stares of the other vendors bore through her back, and she knew they listened to every word. She longed to disappear into the shadows and never return.

When Lillian was young, she walked home with her mother along the dusty dirt road from Manorhamilton. They passed a girl going the other way who didn't like Lillian and Lillian didn't like her either. The girl scowled and raised a fist. Lillian's mother told Lillian to not do anything except ignore the faery-touched girl. Of course, Lillian didn't listen. She spoke a spell under her breath for the bramble they passed to send a vine out to trip the girl. Lillian's mother noticed and spelled Lillian's mouth shut until they arrived home. But Lillian noted the girl's fall and scream and snickered. Her mother turned towards her. "You're evil, you know." Lillian shrugged. She had listened to it every day from her mother.

Today, she caught it from all directions.

Now, as she and her girls continued along the market street, Lillian bowed her head, hair hanging in her face, hiding her eyes. The rumors had spread like wildfire, and now she was an outcast in town. But Lillian was no stranger to being ostracized - she had suffered her grandmother's warnings all her life. She had kept everyone at arm's length, knowing that she was a danger to those around her. She lifted her head, her girls by her side.

Rumors never go away, and they were a way of life in town. But this one was different, even dangerous. She had to stop it before it got out of hand. She had a family to take care of, and she would do whatever it took to protect them, even if it meant a dance with the devil himself.

But the weight of the stares and whispers felt heavier than ever. Lillian longed to flee back to the safety of her simple hut, but she knew she had to face this. She straightened her spine and pushed forward, determined to clear her name and show the townsfolk that she was no servant of the devil. She approached her regular customers, the ones who trusted her, and offered them her teas and remedies, not able to avoid a few hesitant glances and averted eyes.

At least she made money to add to the rent jar. Sean would receive his monthly pay tomorrow. He made little since the landlord argued he let him pay lower rent besides his pay. Landlords always took advantage. That's how they got richer. That's how the system worked.

Chapter Fifteen

Sean trudged to the turnip field he had labored on the day before. It felt like an endless expanse, with more turnips than one could fathom, thriving in the rich soil. The work was grueling, but its monotony allowed him to find solace in reciting bible verses to himself.

"Hey there, Sean. Another day, another turnip," greeted Matthew, his fellow turnip cutter, who employed his remarkable voice to sing as he toiled.

"True that," Sean replied.

Matthew continued, "I heard quite the tale about your wife at the pub last night. They said she danced naked by the river with the devil himself, horns and all. Someone even tried to shoot her, and she vanished only to reappear further down the river." He chuckled until Sean's fist connected with his face.

Sean stood over Matthew, poised for another blow. "Find that amusing, do you? Why would anyone talk about my wife that way?"

Matthew sprawled on the ground, using his hands to shield his face. "No, mate. I'm just telling you what I heard. Sorry."

Regret washed over Sean, and he extended his hand in apology. "I'm sorry I hit you. It angered me to hear you laugh about that. No one wants their wife spoken of like that."

Matthew declined Sean's hand, instead opting to rise on his own. "I wasn't laughing at Lillian. She's a good person and an exceptional healer."

Embarrassment and guilt flushed Sean's cheeks. "I'm sorry. I hope you can forgive me. There's no excuse for hitting you. I've struck no one before." He walked away, venting his anger on the far side of the field.

The turnips flew while Sean pondered his situation. He had warned Lillian that he would leave if the rumors continued. Yet, each time, the stories seemed to grow wilder. Still, he loved Lillian and Stella. The thought of leaving them behind weighed on him. He had longed for a family like this, but now he questioned how far he could endure Lillian's trouble-making tendencies. Were there no bounds to her paranoia and vindictiveness? He asserted her fears were baseless, and revenge was immoral. But the more he pressed, the more she pushed back. And now, he admitted, he had reached his breaking point.

Sean left the field without a word to anyone. He departed work early, knowing he wouldn't return.

Upon reaching home, he packed his belongings into the same bag as before—his clothes, personal items, and even the cross hanging on the wall. Securing the drawstring, he contemplated his next move.

If he ventured the main road, someone might inquire about the bag or question why he wasn't working. On this road, everyone knew each other's business. Instead, he crossed the neighbor's fields behind the house, aiming to reach the forest. He sought solace in returning to his parents' home, where at least the love was genuine and not tainted by witchcraft. It broke his heart to leave Stella.

Thoughts of his family guided him as Sean set out on the journey home, knowing they would say, "I told you so." He preferred that to lying beside someone he suspected of being a witch. Would he ever be certain he had truly loved her or it resulted from her supposed witchcraft?

As he walked, another figure crossed his mind—Grace. She had shown an interest in him before, and he hoped she wasn't like her sister, ensnared by witchcraft. She had warned him about Lillian, and he considered the possibility of pursuing a future with her. He altered his course, heading towards Manorhamilton.

When Lillian returned home, she noticed the front door looked different on the top, like it has a sheen on it. As she got closer, she realized the orb weaver spider she fed bugs to had spun a web back and forth across the top of the door. She could walk under, but she was sure Sean would not. The air inside seemed different when she opened the door. Mary ran in circles, laughing. Lillian's eyes scanned the room and stopped at the empty spot on the wall where the cross no longer hung.

Lillian approached her bed and scrambled through their basket, not finding any of Sean's clothes. Everything gone. She plopped on their bed. What would she tell the girls? Or anyone else? How would she heal her heart?

Lillian had no remedy for a broken heart or any affairs of the heart. She couldn't make anyone fall in love or fall out of love. It was beyond her powers. Because it was the greatest power of all. And she didn't respect it. Now she had lost the love of her life. Sean had made her feel invincible. How would she manage her rage and suspicions of everyone around her without him?

This was the wheat farmer's fault. If he wouldn't have told that tall tale, Sean wouldn't have left. She would take care of the farmer this very night after she put the girls to bed.

She fixed dinner and set the table for four.

"When is Da coming home?" Stella kept looking at the door as if that would make him materialize.

Lillian composed her voice to hide the despair she felt in his absence. "Da had to go track a big cat, a lynx, that was seen nearby before it can get any of the livestock. He will be back soon." Lillian hated lying to Stella. Such an innocent, sweet child did not deserve that.

Mary yelled, "Da's gone!" Lillian stared at the blank spot on the wall where his cross had hung.

Stella slapped her hand on the table. "He's not. Da's coming back." She shoved her bowl of potatoes and milk, pushed back her chair, and ran to her bed. The bed slid a little from the force of her throwing herself on it. She sobbed, head buried into the pillow.

Lillian gave Mary a stern look when she laughed. Didn't Sean consider how this would affect Stella? Lillian worried about how Mary acted from her laughing circle to her sudden announcement, as if she had knowledge of his whereabouts. Mary was a strange child; Lillian admitted it, though, not to Sean, who didn't have a fondness for her.

That night, near the wheat farmer's field hidden by the brambles along the road from his dogs, she placed the bowl of water she brought on the ground. Lillian lifted her arms, spoke a mirror spell to allow her to see what was happening in the field from her position.

As moonbeams grace this sacred ground,
Let droplets form, a surface found.
In every droplet, see the light,
Reflecting images, clear and bright.
So mote it be!

Lillian spoke another spell, bringing the wind into her hands.

Whirl and twirl, the dance shall start,
Let nature's breath be your art.
With hands outstretched, you shall command,
The winds of time at your demand.
So mote it be!

As she moved her hands, she orchestrated a pattern for the wind to flatten the wheat in one swirling direction and another until she had the pattern she wanted. Then she faced another part of the field and did the same. And once more.

In the mirrored reflection, she saw the intricate Dara knot, a symbol of strength representing the root system of an ancient oak. A warning to others of her strength, power, and endurance. No one would see the knot unless they climbed the hill at the end of his land where the stream was or got on the roof of the farmer's house. It didn't matter as long as she damaged the wheat. That was the goal. Now the farmer can tell another tale of how he starved one year because of a freak wind storm.

Lillian walked home, chin jutted out and a hard smile until she reached her sod house, where only she and her children lived. There was no one sharing her bed. It would be cold and lonely when she climbed in.

The next morning when Lillian and the girls came out the door, Matthew walked through the gate. She took a deep breath and readied the lie she would tell.

"Good morning, Matthew."

Matthew took off his cap, crushing it in his hands. He sported a black eye. "I came looking for Sean. We had a falling out the other day and then he left work early without a word to nobody. The landlord told me to come here to inquire on my way to work."

"Oh. Did my Sean hit you?" It was like a rock fell in her stomach. Sean was never one to use physical force; he used dead silence and absence.

"Aye. I said something I heard about you and I shouldn't have said it."

Time for the lie. "I'm sorry about that. He said nothing before he left to track a lynx that appeared in our yard. I haven't seen him since."

Matthew furrowed his brows. "He has a rifle, and he hunts?"

Lillian started for the gate in a move to show him the conversation was over. "I'll send him over when he comes back. It's good to see you."

Matthew turned to leave. "Aye. Same." He replaced his hat and continued on his way to the landlord's fields.

Lillian led the girls through the gate and latched it. A turn of her hand and a few words ensured no one would enter except herself. That was for any too curious for their own good, especially the magistrate. There were far too many things in the house that the authorities would use against her. She would make it hard for anyone to stand up against her. Trust didn't exist for Lillian.

It was time to make sales to guarantee she paid the rent without Sean. She feared the landlord would raise the rent because of Sean not working the fields. The thought that he could evict her for a better tenant was her greatest worry and kept her awake for hours. She was exploring a plan to curse the house to make that impossible. There were many ways to do that, but which was the best? She might only get one shot at preserving the roof over her and her children's heads.

Chapter Sixteen

Two weeks slipped by, their passage marked by an air of palpable tension that gripped the town. Lillian's missing husband, Sean, cast a dark shadow over her every step. Whispers wafted through the streets, winding their way from ear to ear like malicious tendrils. The tales grew wilder and wilder, painting Lillian as a woman steeped in sorcery and darkness.

There were townsfolk who claimed she had transformed Sean into a minuscule mouse, caged and hidden away in her home. Others wove stories of a furious fit of rage that had swallowed him whole, leaving naught but a void in his place. No longer did the townsfolk seek solace in her potent remedies, nor did they dare engage her in conversation. Lillian became an outcast, shunned and granted a wide berth by all.

Stella wept bitter tears, her friends seeking refuge behind the protective veil of their mothers' dresses. Fear had woven itself into the fabric of their lives, tainting even the innocence of childhood.

Patrick Reynolds, the magistrate, grabbed her upper arm. "Come to my office."

Lillian had no choice, his grip tight. He dragged her and the children into his office, flanked by two stern guards who stood as silent sentinels.

Once inside, Patrick sat in his chair behind an oak desk and wasted no time. His piercing gaze bore into Lillian, the weight of suspicion heavy upon his features. Words spilled forth, questions tumbling from his lips like shards of ice.

"Where is Sean?" he asked.

Lillian's voice quivered with her practiced lie. "A lynx attacked our cow, and Sean tracked it into the fields behind our house. I expected him to return, but he never did. I fear something has befallen him."

Patrick's scrutiny intensified as he probed. "And what of the farmer's field? What knowledge do you possess of this matter?"

Lillian met his gaze and twirled a bit of hair around her finger. "A Púca, sir. Someone must have disturbed the spirits, perhaps by eating overripe blackberries." She paused, knowing well the tales of Púcas, a shapeshifting trickster spirit, that enticed unsuspecting souls to ride upon their backs.

A flash of incredulity crossed Patrick's face, his head cocked. "Ha. A mere myth," he uttered. He cleared his throat. "Recall the conversation we had in your home, Lillian. The accusations of cursing a newborn, the cow's sour milk, the barren fields that yield no sustenance. Now, this town suffers from one perpetual sickness after another, and yet, on that same day, you conveniently hold the cure within your basket." He stood and pitched over the desk, leaning on the palms of his hands. He raised his voice and asked, "Do you sleep with the devil? Dance with him in the veil of night, unclothed? Do you worship the very essence of evil?"

Startled by the sudden onslaught of accusations, Lillian's voice trembled and she leaned back as far as she could. "The farmer fabricated that tale when he found me admiring rare orchids by the creek bed. He craved attention. Perhaps it was his words that disturbed the Púca. As for your other allegations, I assure you, I have no dealings with the devil. I swear it."

Patrick's eyes narrowed. "And what of your husband, Lillian? He vanished without a trace."

A knot formed in Lillian's stomach, and she squirmed in her chair.

"He hunted the lynx that had been lurking around our home," Lillian said, tears streaming along her cheeks. "But he never returned."

"No one else has spotted or seen tracks of a lynx!"

Lillian watched her hands shake in her lap. "I don't understand why no one else has seen the creature in the area."

A glint of cold resolve flickered in Patrick's eyes. "Guards! Put her in a cell," he commanded, his voice booming. The weight of his accusations, fueled by the town's suspicions, seemed to seal Lillian's fate.

As the guards moved to apprehend her, a piercing cry rang through the room. "No! No! You can't have her. Mama!" It was Mary, her small body quivering.

Patrick's gaze turned upon the child, his features hardening further. "Give me the bairn," he demanded, reaching out to snatch her from Lillian's grasp.

Mary's resistance erupted like a storm. She kicked and flailed, her tiny fists striking against the magistrate's imposing figure. "You are out of your mind!" she screamed, her voice full of righteous indignation.

Undeterred by the child's defiance, Patrick motioned to his assistant. "Take them to my home," he said, a glimmer of satisfaction playing across his face.

"Please! My brother is in Manorhamilton. Send word so he may come for them," Lillian pleaded.

"My wife will care for the children until their uncle arrives. If he doesn't appear within a reasonable amount of time, I'm sure the church will extend its benevolent hand and provide shelter for them in the orphanage."

Stella sobbed, crouched in the room's corner, shaking her head.

Lillian's anguish filled the room as she pleaded, "Not the church, please!"

But her pleas fell upon deaf ears, drowned out by the magistrate's unwavering resolve. His eyes remained fixed on her, his voice steady and cold. "I will find your brother, Lillian. The children have done no harm and deserve a home free from the taint of witchcraft. Tell me, is your brother also entwined in such darkness?"

Lillian shook her head and accepted her fate as the guards led her away. Her shoulders slumped, and her head bowed, a portrait of defeated resilience. What else could they strip away from her? In this moment of despair, the only solace remaining was the power coursing through her veins, a flame no mortal men could extinguish.

Lillian's days in the shadowy cell stretched on, marked by the rhythmic scuttling of rats that served as her only companions. The monotony of her confinement compelled her to practice her magick, weaving her power around the rodents, captivating them in a dance of her own making. It was a futile attempt to wile away time, a miserable bid to find solace amidst the gloom.

The guards' entrance presented a stark disruption to her solitary routine. Lillian seized the opportunity to declare her desperate plea. "I want to see my children," she cried out, her voice echoing off the cold stone walls.

The first guard, his face hardened by years of enforcing authority, paid her no mind. He said, "You have a visitor. Keep it brief," while he swung open the creaking door.

Hope flickered in Lillian's eyes as she waited, anticipating the joyful arrival of her beloved daughters. Yet, to her dismay, it was her brother, James, who walked through the threshold. He was the last remaining link to her shattered family, the only one who still believed in her despite his limited understanding of her powers.

Seating himself on the edge of her narrow bed, James shook his head while scratching his jaw. He said, his voice rushed, hands splayed out, "How did you end up here? They're accusing you of murdering an infant, for God's sake."

Lillian lifted her weary gaze and gave an impatient snort. Through gritted teeth, she said, "I didn't kill any baby. The child was dead before I even arrived to assist the mother. I saved her life, but no one wants to listen." Her fists pounded the cot.

James nodded. "And what about this charge of obscenity? It sounds absurd. How could they accuse you of such a thing?"

A heavy sigh escaped Lillian's lips, her shoulders slumped. "I went to admire rare orchids by the creek bed at night. I didn't bother dressing, only wore a chemise, thinking no one would witness my solitary excursion. But the farmer's dogs grew restless, and when he investigated, he claimed to have seen me dancing with the Devil in the nude. He said I vanished when he fired his weapon," she recounted. She dropped her head in her hands.

James furrowed his face, his disbelief clear. "And they believed him? I would deem anyone spreading such tales touched in the head. The faeries must have bewitched him."

Lillian straightened, a glimmer of gratitude flickering in her eyes. "From that moment, the rumors spiraled out of control, each story more outlandish than the last."

A surge of emotion overwhelmed Lillian and she wept. Tears spilled over her face, spreading on the fabric of her dress. "And Sean... he couldn't bear the weight of the rumors. He abandoned me and our daughters without a word," she said, hands clenched into fists.

James enveloped his sister in a comforting embrace, offering solace in the face of her shattered world. He vowed, "I will find someone to represent you in court. I will search for the girls and bring them home. I won't rest until we can secure your release."

Lillian clung to her brother, cherishing the steadfast presence he represented in the storm. As the only boy in the family, he had assumed the mantle of responsibility when their father had vanished without a trace.

"There's something else you should know," James said, his voice flat, the look in his eyes distant. "Sean came to see Grace."

Lillian stood tall, her hands planted on her hips, her defiance simmering beneath her anguish. A bitter truth pierced her heart. "He can have her. Neither of them believes in family, only themselves."

James nodded, lips pressed tight into a grimace. His gaze locked on Lillian's, his unwavering support shining through. Without a word, he rose and approached the door, knocking to signal his departure. The guard opened it, and as James stepped out, Lillian called after him, her voice full of emotion.

"Thank you, James," she uttered, her words hanging in the stale air of the cell. But the door slammed shut, drowning out her gratitude. Undeterred, she repeated her heartfelt appreciation louder. "Thank you!"

Yet, even as her words echoed into silence, a flicker of hope tried to ignite within her. Lillian couldn't afford to raise her expectations, to subject herself to further disappointment. Wrapped in her grief, she returned to the company of the rats, their beady eyes serving as solemn witnesses to her plight.

But as she continued her silent communion with the rats, the echoes of her daughters' laughter and the warmth of James's embrace served as beacons in the abyss.

Time seemed to stretch, each passing moment fueling Lillian's determination. She resolved to hold on to her powers, her resilience, the ember of hope that still flickered within her. Deep down, she was aware of her power, a strength that would withstand any storm, even when it felt like the entire world was against her.

CHAPTER SEVENTEEN

JAMES TRUDGED THROUGH THE narrow streets of the town, his eyes darting from one law office to another. Each door he approached shut in his face, the lawyers within refusing to spare him even a moment of their precious time. Dismissed and discarded, he felt the sting of rejection. One more office remained.

James hesitated at the threshold of the lawyer's office. He couldn't afford to be turned away. He took a deep breath, steeling himself for the encounter that lay ahead, and pushed open the door, its creaking hinges protesting his intrusion.

Inside, the air hung heavy in the aromas of aged leather and stale cigar smoke. The lawyer, his face etched by time and cynicism, looked up from his cluttered desk, eyes narrowed. James squared his shoulders, refusing to cave in to the lawyer's scowl.

"I need someone," James said, his voice steady but urgent, "to represent my sister. She's ensnared in a twisted web of accusations—charges of witchcraft and obscenity that defy reason."

The lawyer's lips curled into a sneer, as though he had heard similar pleas a thousand times before. "No one in their right mind will touch that case," he retorted, his words like a sword unsheathed, ready to strike any flicker of hope. "Get out of here before you waste any more of my precious time."

But James refused to yield to the lawyer's biting rejection. He knew the battle that awaited him, the uphill climb against prejudice and ignorance. He wouldn't allow his sister's fate to be sealed by a society eager to condemn without understanding.

James met the lawyer's scowl, leaning in, jaw set. "She deserves a fair trial," James asserted, his voice defiant. "Just as any other person accused of a crime. She's my sister, and I won't abandon her in this hour of need."

The air crackled with tension as the lawyer rose from his chair, a physical presentation of the wall of resistance James had encountered all day. The man's menacing presence loomed, radiating a ruthless aura.

With a swift, purposeful stride, the lawyer circled the desk, closing the distance between them. He reached out, his hand an iron vice that clamped onto James' shoulder, attempting to push him out the door. "Save yourself the grief," the lawyer spat, his voice derisive. "Go home. Forget about this foolish crusade."

James stumbled back but regained his footing, refusing to be thrown aside. He straightened his spine, thrust his chest out. He inhaled deep through his nose and exhaling through his mouth, calming himself.

James refused to surrender, fueled by the love for his sister. Determination burned within him, a fierce flame that fueled his relentless pursuit. But he had run out of options. He backed away and exit the office. He shoved his hands into his pockets while heading down the street.

Under his breath, James unleashed a torrent of curses, aimed at his brother-in-law, Sean. He berated him for his weakness, for abandoning his wife in this wretched and unforgiving circumstance. The curses continued, accusing Sean of being a wretched father, leaving his own children without the guidance and care of both parents. "Bad cess to you, Sean. May you find the bees but miss the honey." Yet Sean was not the sole target of James' ire.

Lillian, his sister, came under the weight of his curses as well. He condemned her as paranoid and stubborn, blaming her for putting her innocent children at risk. Bitter words flowed from his lips, condemning her for her choices, for the perilous path she had chosen. "The bad deed returns on the bad-deed doer." But the curses did not cease there, for James directed his anger at their mother and aunts as well. He blasted them for forsaking Lillian when she needed their guidance the most, leaving her adrift and vulnerable. "May they have an itch, but no nails for scratching."

Amidst his fervent curses, James could not escape the shadow of self-blame. He berated himself for not paying attention enough, for failing to stay on top of Lillian's ever-changing situation. He knew Lillian and Sean had lied to him about the reasons behind their frequent moves, especially the last one. Regret gnawed at his conscience, tormenting him for his lack of insight. "It serves me right."

Though the curses brought him no solace, they served as an exercise for his restless mind. James, determination in his eyes, stood before the magistrate's grand house and knocked.

A servant answered. "Can I help you?"

James crushed his hat in his hands. "My name is James. My nieces are here and I want to take them home."

The man rolled his eyes as he scanned James. "Wait here."

A woman dressed in the latest fashions presented herself at the door. "I am pleased you are here to retrieve them. The oldest is polite and quiet. That other one is a beast. I won't miss her." She turned and nodded.

"Uncle James!" Stella and Mary exclaimed in unison as they raced through the door, their tiny voices joyful and eager. They wrapped their small arms around his legs, their embraces tightening until he kneeled to meet them. Without hesitation, they threw themselves into his waiting arms. It was a joyful reunion after months apart.

James left the magistrate's house, the girls holding onto each of his hands as they embarked on the journey to their home on Leitrim Road. The countryside stretched out before them, bathed in the soft hues of twilight. Along the way, the girls' voices carried on the wind, their sweet tones intertwining with the gentle rustle of leaves and the distant melodies of nature. Their innocent chatter filled the air, like the delicate notes of a song that echoed through the hidden corners of their hearts.

"Uncle James," Stella said, her voice full of hope, "when is Mama coming back? Will she be home soon?"

James paused, his steps faltering for a moment as he gazed at Stella's wide, curious eyes. It was a dagger to his own wounded heart. He yearned to shield them from the harsh reality that loomed overhead, to preserve their innocence and protect the fragile wings of their hope.

The weight of silence settled upon them, a palpable reminder of the painful truth he dared not utter. He kneeled, his eyes meeting Stella's, and brushed a stray lock of hair behind her ear. His voice, tempered by sorrow and love, and an honesty he could not deny.

"Stella," he said, his voice soft yet regretful, "I wish I could give you the answer you long to hear. I wish I could promise you that your mother will return soon, that this darkness will dissipate, and your lives will be as they once were."

Mary, the younger of the two, clung to James's leg, her eyes wide and searching. She was too young to grasp the weight of their situation, but her mother's absence was a palpable void in her life, an ache she couldn't comprehend.

"But sometimes," James continued, his voice emotional, "life takes us down paths we never expected. Sometimes the road ahead has obstacles that seem insurmountable. Your mother is facing a battle, a fight for justice and truth, and it may take time. It may be a long journey."

The girls exchanged glances, their innocent faces outlined in confusion and longing. James pulled them both into an embrace, enveloping them in a cocoon of warmth and love.

"But know this," James whispered, "no matter how long it takes, no matter the outcome, we will walk this path together. You are not alone, my precious ones."

As they continued their journey, the path before him seemed less daunting, his steps infused in a renewed sense of purpose. This was no place for them to witness their mother's unjust persecution and have such a dreadful accusation hanging over their heads.

A glimmer of hope flickered in the darkness that plagued his mind. James had received a job offer in Pennsylvania. In that distant land, he envisioned a new life, free from the insidious rumors that tarnished his family's name. Perhaps his suspicions about his mother, aunts, and even his sisters being witches turned out to be less absurd than he thought. Lillian's emotions—her rage, mistrust, and vindictiveness—made her become a victim of her eccentricities.

James decided on a course of action, his resolve hardening within him. Tomorrow, he would pen a letter accepting the job offer and begin preparations for their journey to America. He had been diligent in saving money for this eventuality, even enough to cover two more tickets. A cousin of his was already working in the Pennsylvania mines, and he hoped his wife would watch the girls while he worked.

Yet, as he pondered the course of action, a piercing ache gripped his chest. The anguish of leaving his sister behind to endure her torment alone tore at his soul. But he had a duty, a solemn obligation to protect her children, to shield them from the monstrous accusations that lurked within the shadows of this town. Tomorrow, he would gather the strength to explain his plans and admit his inability to aid Lillian's cause in court.

A heavy shroud of sorrow descended upon James as he envisaged the approaching day. He would orchestrate the girls' last conversation with their mother tomorrow. It would be a sad day, one he wished he could circumvent, but the welfare of his nieces was the paramount concern.

Along the way towards their home on Leitrim Road, James steeled himself for the trials that lay ahead. The unknown expanse of the Atlantic Ocean beckoned, promising a new beginning and respite from the persecution that had plagued them. Yet, the ache within his heart reminded him of the sacrifices to be made, of the price that would be paid.

The sun dipped below the horizon, casting its last rays upon their path. James whispered a prayer for strength, for his sister's deliverance, and for the resilience of his nieces. Tomorrow, he would embark on a journey that would shape their futures, leaving behind a dark situation and cling to the fragile hope of a brighter tomorrow.

Lillian, in her dim, solitary cell, stroked a flickering flame on her finger. Time seemed to stretch, punctuated only by the hollow echoes of her thoughts. Missing her daughters left a jagged wound in her heart that refused to heal.

The heavy sound of the guard's footsteps cut through the suffocating silence. Lillian's hopes soared, yearning for the sight of her beloved daughters. She extinguished the flame on her finger, a flicker of anticipation dancing within her. "You have visitors."

As the door swung open, James entered. Stella and Mary rushed past him, their laughter echoing through the hallway as they ran into their mother's open arms. Their joyous voices echoed through the cold, stone walls, a symphony of innocence that for a moment washed away the darkness.

"Mama! We missed you," Stella exclaimed, her voice exuding a joyous love that would melt even the coldest of hearts.

Mary's impatience spilled forth. "When are you coming home?" she demanded, her little foot stomping.

Lillian's smile, fragile yet radiant, enveloped her youngest daughter as she pulled her close. "I don't know, my darling. They think I'm a terrible person, but remember, their thoughts do not define us."

Mary, ever defiant, placed her hands on her hips, eyes blazing. "They are out of their minds! Faery touched," she declared, her words a testament to her unwavering belief in her mother.

But Stella remained silent, her gaze fixed upon Lillian. In her eyes, the weight of the world seemed to settle, as if the ordeal had aged her beyond her tender years. Lillian's heart broke at the sight, but she knew she had to stay strong for her daughters, to shield them from the storm that raged within her own soul.

Drawing Stella close, Lillian whispered her instructions, her voice both urgent and full of a mother's unwavering love. "I need you to take my necklace and put it in your apron pocket. And when you get home, place it and my special book in a bag. I want you to say the spell we learned together, the one that makes it visible only to you and Mary. Keep it safe, my brave soldier, and protect your sister." She removed the invisible jewelry from her neck and placed it in Stella's palm.

Tears welled in Stella's eyes as she nodded, her grip on the necklace tightening. Lillian caught the fleeting moment when their gazes locked. The unspoken understanding between mother and daughter threatening to unravel their resolve. But Lillian held back her tears, her emotions welling beneath the surface. *Not in front of the girls.*

Stella slipped the necklace in her apron pocket, head down, tears dripping on the floor. She scooted her shoe over the wet spots on the floor as if to hide the evidence.

James took a seat beside Lillian, his hand finding hers. Mary nestled herself against her mother's side, seeking solace in their connection.

"You won't like what I have to say," James said, grimacing, his gaze flickering between Lillian and her daughters. "I've exhausted every avenue, but I couldn't find someone to represent you. A fair trial is out of reach. The outcome has already been determined, I'm sorry to say."

Lillian took a cleansing breath and met her brother's eyes. She articulated each word. "Protect my daughters, James. Do what's best for them. I will protect myself."

A soft smile graced James's lips, a fleeting moment of respite in the face of adversity. "I won't let them down. I have a job offer in America. A good job as a mining foreman. We have our cousin, Robert, there. I'm hoping his wife will care for the girls while I'm working."

"I like his wife. She will be perfect." Lillian squeezed her brother's hand.

James's brows lifted in surprise, a flicker of admiration crossing his features. "You've always been stronger than you give yourself credit for," James said, a mix of pride and sadness in his voice. "I should have been there more, Lillian. I should have protected you. Sean was not strong enough for you."

Lillian's hand tightened around her brother's, empathizing with his pain. "You've always been there when it mattered most, James. You've been my rock. Sean loved me and that was enough...until it wasn't." She shrugged her shoulders. "Can't blame him. I have my problems."

James nudged her with his shoulder. "Na. Where did you get that idea?" He laughed and Lillian joined him.

Amid their shared resolve, Mary's scowl turned into a look of curiosity. "What's so funny?" she asked, her eyes flitting between her mother and uncle.

Lillian's laughter rang out, a brief respite from the heavy mood that lingered around them. "You are, my clever girl." Her voice wove both amusement and affection.

Mary pouted. "I am not funny! I am smart," she retorted.

Uncle James pulled her close, his voice gentle yet firm. "You're right, Mary. You are smart, smarter than most. And that's why we're going on a trip."

A spark of excitement ignited within Stella's eyes, her voice filled with anticipation. "Where are we going, Uncle James?"

Lillian's heart was heavy as she regarded the dilemma of shielding her daughters from the cruelties of life or giving them hope for a better tomorrow. She looked at her brother, pleading for guidance.

James's gaze met Lillian's, a shared understanding passing between them. The truth would only cause more pain. "We're going to America," he said.

Mary's excitement bubbled over, causing her to bounce on her feet. "We're going to America!" she exclaimed, her joy infectious.

Lillian shook her head, knowing that the truth would soon come crashing. How could she explain to her daughters that she would not be going?

"We're going in a few days."

As the excitement lingered in the air, Lillian's heart felt heavy with the weight of her impending challenge. She knew she couldn't be with her daughters, couldn't share in the journey they were about to embark upon. The truth was too harsh a burden for them to bear at this moment.

She took a deep breath, mustering the strength within her, and turned to her daughters. "Listen to Uncle James, my darlings," she whispered, her voice choked. "He will keep you safe. And remember, I will always be with you in spirit, watching over you from afar."

The unshed tears in Stella's eyes threatened to spill over as she nodded, taking on the burden of responsibility.

Mary clung to Lillian, her small hands gripping. "Promise you'll come, Mommy," she pleaded. The innocence in her voice tore at Lillian's heart.

Lillian's gaze met her daughter's, an unspoken promise flickering between them. "I promise, my sweet girl," she whispered, her voice carrying the weight of an unbreakable vow. "I will join you. Until then, be brave and take care of each other."

As they embraced one last time, Lillian wondered what the future held. What sacrifices she would need to make? Would redemption come to pass?

Anguish washed over Lillian as James led her daughters away, their footsteps growing fainter and fainter with each passing moment. She knew this was the price she had to pay to guarantee their safety, to give them a chance at a life free from the shadows that haunted her.

Alone in her cell, Lillian sank to her knees, tears streaming down her face. The ache within her heart intensified, a poignant reminder of the love she held for her daughters. She whispered a silent plea to the forces unseen to guide and protect her children on their journey.

CHAPTER EIGHTEEN

LILLIAN'S SENSES EMERGED FROM the clutches of sleep as a voice wove its way into her consciousness, shattering the veil of dreams. During her attempts to blink away the remnants of slumber, she found herself face-to-face with a figure of imposing stature. Clad in black, the stranger exuded an aura of authority, his commanding presence underlined by a hooded cloak draping his broad shoulders. A suit of armor adorned his chest, and a pistol strapped to his hip. Stirred from her repose, Lillian scrambled to an upright position, her bleary eyes striving to comprehend the situation at hand.

"I am the Inquisitor," the enigmatic man declared with an air of formality, his voice carrying a weighty resonance. "The Church has summoned me to oversee your trial. You will undergo a series of tests designed to find out whether you are truly a witch or imposter." His hand gravitated towards the butt of his gun, a subtle but palpable threat lingering in the gesture.

Patrick, the magistrate, arrived to stand beside the Inquisitor. His presence was now far less foreboding alongside the Inquisitor. "Indeed, let us begin without delay." He rubbed his hands together.

The Inquisitor leaned forward, lowering his head, his eyes narrowed, their steely gaze piercing Lillian's own. "You shall recite the Lord's Prayer," he said. "Surely, you know this sacred verse?"

A sly smirk graced Lillian's lips, a defiance veiled beneath her expression. "Of course," she said, hands held loose behind her back. "The Lord's Prayer is a familiar refrain, is it not?" She stood tall and clasped her hands together in front of her, palms pressed. "Our Father, who art in heaven, hallowed be thy name. Thy kingdom come, thy will be done, on earth as it is in heaven," she recited, her voice clear. "Give us this day our daily bread and forgive us our debts as we forgive our debtors. And lead us not into temptation, but deliver us from evil. For thine is the kingdom, and the power, and the glory, forever. Amen." Her head arched backward, a tight smile aimed at the Inquisitor, her defiance simmering just beneath the surface.

"Excellent," Patrick exclaimed. "She recited it flawlessly. You believed she could not utter the prayer if she were a witch. The devil himself would never allow such purity."

The Inquisitor swiveled his gaze toward the magistrate, brows furrowed and lips curled into a display of displeasure. "It seems the Devil is becoming more knowledgeable about our methods of uncovering his presence," he said. "We have further tests."

The Inquisitor's movement seized, frozen in place as if trapped within an invisible vise. A momentary lapse in his stride, accompanied by a fit of coughing, compelled him to retrieve a handkerchief from his person. As he brought the fabric to his mouth, blood tainted its pristine surface, an alarming sight that bore witness to his affliction. After wiping away the evidence of his ailment, he steadied himself, his voice wavering. "I shall return," he declared, his cape swirling around his legs as he spun to face the door.

Before the Inquisitor could take another step, Lillian's voice cut through the air. "I can offer you aid against this wasting," she said, her words reaching the man's ears like a whisper from the depths of forbidden knowledge.

The Inquisitor froze in his tracks, his eyes widening in disbelief. "It is God's will," he retorted. "I shall not seek help from the Devil."

A cryptic smile played upon Lillian's lips as she inclined her head, pondering the limitations imposed upon the faithful. It's strange how they reject the existence of magick, attributing everything to divine intervention. Miracles are nothing but magick themselves. "So be it," she said, shaking her head. "You would rather succumb to choking on your own blood while prayers to your god go unanswered."

Without a word, the Inquisitor resumed his solemn march. The guard stepped aside to allow the towering figure passage. As he and the magistrate exited the confines of the cell, the heavy door groaned, sealing Lillian within its chilly embrace once more.

Ean tapped at the windowsill and ruffled his feathers. It caught the magistrate's attention.

When the magistrate paused, Lillian drew in a sharp breath, her features hardening. Crossing her arms over her chest, she stared down the corridor through narrowed eyes, a flicker of anticipation dancing within her gaze. "You have taken everything from me," she whispered, "everything except what flows through me. And that, my dear magistrate, you cannot take away. No matter what torments you inflict upon me."

The magistrate lingered for a moment, his gaze held. "You are a stubborn woman," he said. He gave her a nod before he turned and followed in the Inquisitor's wake, leaving Lillian to her solitude.

Lillian exhaled a heavy sigh, a glimmer of relief washing over her. Alone, she stood amidst the silence and shadows, her spirit unyielding, braced for the trials that awaited her. For she knew that within her lay a power that defied their comprehension, a force waiting to be unleashed upon the world.

Lillian bid her time; her resolve was unshaken, her heart aflame with the flickering embers of defiance. Lillian awaited the dawning of her liberation, aware that the trials ahead would mold her into something more than the sum of her shattered life.

The next day arrived, accompanied by the jingle of keys and the heavy footsteps of the guard. In his wake trailed an old woman, her face etched with lines of weariness and trepidation. Not a word passed between her and Lillian as she approached, the weight of her duty palpable in the air. Grasping Lillian's arm, the woman twirled her around, untying the knots that bound Lillian's apron.

Indignant fury surged through Lillian's veins, compelling her to push the woman away. "What do you think you're doing?" she demanded.

The woman, unfazed by Lillian's resistance, tightened her grip and offered a gruff explanation. "I'm merely carrying out orders to strip you to your chemise. They are going to dunk you in the river."

Lillian tightened her shawl around her shoulders, her eyes blazing as she yanked away. "If they wish to see me disrobed, I am more than capable of accomplishing that myself. Be gone, old woman."

A sinister smile played on Lillian's lips. "What form should I turn you into?" she mused aloud, her words wicked. "Perhaps a rat, though that would be too commonplace. Or a toad...how dreadfully dull. Ah, yes, a fly. An incessantly bothersome fly, swatted at and ensnared within a spider's web. Spun up and suffocated, a delectable dinner."

The woman staggered back, her trembling fingers pressing against her parted lips in a mixture of shock and terror. She turned to the guard, her voice quivering. "Release me from this place. I expect proper compensation for enduring such horrors."

Unlocking the cell door, the guard obeyed her desperate plea. The woman bolted out and fled into the dark corridor. The resounding clang of the door slamming shut enclosed Lillian within its oppressive confines.

Once free from her dress, Lillian sat on the cold stone floor, her legs pulled up against her chest in the saffron-colored cocoon of her chemise. *They can drag me out. I will not make it easy.* As time went on, her fortitude grew stronger and stronger, forming into an unstoppable force that could withstand anything they threw at her.

"Bring her!" a resounding command echoed from the hall, causing the guard to approach the cell door. His keyring jingled as he fumbled with the lock, the sound reverberating within the narrow confines of the cell. Standing over Lillian, he glared at her, his impatience and frustration palpable. "Get up!"

Lillian clung to her position, curling herself tighter into a protective ball. "No," she whispered, her voice a mere breath against the oppressive atmosphere.

Seizing her arm, the guard wrenched Lillian upright, his grip unyielding as he used enough force to yank her body into a limp form, a mere puppet. "Give me a hand!" he barked, casting a desperate glance toward his fellow guard stationed nearby. "She's not coming on her own."

Together, their joint efforts propelled Lillian forward, each step met by her stubborn resistance. The weight of their strength bore upon her, threatening to break her will. But she clung to her defiance, a flicker of determination burned bright within her eyes.

Lillian could hear shouts of "witch" from the crowd gathering outside as they got closer to the front door. Their morbid curiosity fueled the growing tension, adding weight to the impending torment that awaited her.

The guards ushered Lillian into the unforgiving embrace of the open air. In the harsh light of the unforgiving sun, her chemise revealed all. The guards drug her through crowded streets, onlookers following once she had passed. Ean dive-bombed the crowd. It fueled her desire for vengeance.

Upon reaching the river's edge, she spotted the Inquisitor and magistrate on a platform, a stark reminder of her inevitable fate. The crowd gathered, a mixture of pity, morbid fascination, and blind obedience etched upon their faces. Their bluster rose to a dissonant hum. An undercurrent of expectation filled the air.

Lillian's hands, bound behind her back, trembled. The magistrate's voice rang out, amplified by the weight of his conviction. "Proceed! Let the waters judge her."

The ritualistic procedure unfolded, the chilling waters of the River Shannon to serve as both judge and maybe executioner. A rush of dread coursed through Lillian's veins as they trussed her crossways. Her right thumb bound to her left big toe, her left thumb to her right big toe. It was a grotesque display of humiliation and agony, a macabre spectacle designed to test her very essence.

The Archbishop uttered prayers that accompanied the ripples of the water that awaited her. The crowd held its collective breath, their eyes fixed upon Lillian's vulnerable form. It was a moment that would decide her fate, a battle between her indomitable spirit and the twisted notions of righteousness.

As the guards released their hold, Lillian plunged into the icy depths, the river swallowing her with a voracious hunger. Time seemed to stretch, every second a torturous eternity. The weight of the water pressed against her, suffocating her resolve.

Lillian blew air from her mouth into the water to form a protective air bubble, ensuring her survival beneath the depths. It shimmered, a translucent barrier between her and the drowning embrace of the river. And then, in a surge of exhilaration, she felt the buoyant bubble rise against the currents that sought to drown her.

The Inquisitor shouted, ensuring everyone could hear, "She has floated! The water, the essence of baptism and purity, rebelled against her presence. Let this be recorded in the trial records."

The scene fell into a stunned silence as Lillian, drenched and shivering, emerged from the water's surface, bubble broken. Her body hovered just above the river, Lillian delighted her years of practicing levitation paid off.

Gasps of astonishment filled the air as the crowd saw her defiance of the laws of nature and the twisted rituals of the trial. The crowd, once gripped by the certainty of her guilt, now stood witness to a phenomenon that defied their comprehension.

The guards, their hands trembling, hesitated to approach her. Shock and disbelief lay bare on the magistrate's face. Only the Inquisitor stood without emotion crossing his face.

Lillian's voice rang out, commanding attention. "Behold," she said, "the power that lies within, the strength that defies your narrow understanding."

The crowd, once captive to the manipulations of fear and superstition, now stood on the precipice of revelation. Whispers of awe mingled with murmurs of doubt.

Emboldened by her extraordinary feat, Lillian addressed the onlookers. "Do not let ignorance and prejudice control you. Look for the truth that lies beyond the veil of fear and let compassion guide your actions."

Lillian could escape the bonds of the ropes, but she had plans so devious and revengeful, she could wait to enact them when the time was right. The guards undid the crossway bindings and lifted her, her chemise pressed against her body, revealing all. She didn't care. The expressions on the townsfolk buoyed her all the way back to her cold, damp jail cell.

Joy filled Lillian after her victory. She had defied their expectations, shattered their narrow beliefs, and planted a seed of doubt in their hearts.

As she waited for the moment to enact her revenge, the knowledge that she held a power far beyond their comprehension inspired her. The chains of ignorance and prejudice that had bound her were unraveling. She knew her story was far from over, and as she sat on her cot, shawl wrapped around her, a defiant smile played upon her lips.

Chapter Nineteen

THE GUARDS RETURNED. LILLIAN'S heart pounded in her chest as she stood in the shadows of her cell, her body shivering in anticipation. What will they do this time? The flickering torchlight cast eerie shadows across the damp stone walls, heightening the sense of dread that permeated the air. The Inquisitor, a figure of authority and cruelty, entered the room, his air of superiority that made her skin crawl.

"Remove your clothing so I can find your Devil's mark," he commanded as he pointed at her.

Lillian turned away from them, head hung low, and her hands shook as she undid her clothes. She hesitated, her fingers fumbling. She saw the guards' menacing glares left her no choice but to comply.

Bare and vulnerable, her cheeks burned. The Inquisitor's eyes swept over her body, looking for signs of a pact with the devil. Lillian focused on the occasional drip of water echoing in the distance. Ean flapped his wings on the windowsill.

The Inquisitor's gaze fixated on a small birthmark nestled on her shoulder, no larger than a coin. His lips twisted into a sadistic smirk as he pointed. "A mark of Satan," he sneered. Lillian's heart sank, knowing that they would twist any imperfection into proof of her guilt.

Fueled by the defiance that was her nature, she said, "That birth-mark is a testament to my humanity, not a pact with the devil."

The Inquisitor's grip tightened around a vial of holy water plucked from a pocket deep in his cloak. "This is holy water. When it touches the mark, you will feel a burning pain as though if I am dousing the Devil himself."

Lillian braced herself for the pain that awaited her, but resolved to show no signs of weakness. As the cold liquid touched her skin, she fought against the instinct to recoil, channeling every ounce of her willpower to suppress the pain.

To her surprise, the birthmark betrayed none of the sensitivity that they associate with the devil's mark. *I knew it. There is no truth to their beliefs.*

The Inquisitor's face contorted as he released a low growl, his grip on the vial slipping. He continued his examination, but found no other marks to condemn her. Lillian swore she had gleaned a glimmer of doubt in his own eyes. His meticulous search found no pact, no traces of the devil's influence.

Lillian realized she had planted a seed of uncertainty in the very heart of her accusers. A slight smile graced her face as she saw the desperation in his eyes now that his search for a mark of the devil was unsuccessful. True, she was a witch, but she had nothing to do with their devil.

As she stood there, her body still exposed, defiance burned within her, determined to forge her path towards retaliation. The principle of "an eye for an eye" was fundamental to their beliefs, and she awaited her chance to put it into action.

Lillian's heart had sunk when the Inquisitor announced his twisted intentions the day before. He thought the Devil hid her witch's mark but a witch pricker would find it when she didn't feel pain from his pricker.

A chill swept through the air, setting her on edge as she waited for the dreaded pricker from Dublin. Her cell appeared to shrink; the walls closing in around her as she braced herself for the excruciating pain that awaited her. The torchlight in the hall flickered, casting eerie shadows across the stone wall, mirroring the darkness that enveloped her soul.

Hours turned into an agonizing eternity as she waited, her anxiety mounting with each passing minute. The heavy footsteps of the pricker echoed in the corridor, a haunting cadence that resonated deep within her. The door swung open, revealing a figure clothed in worn leather. His eyes gleamed, showing a perverse delight.

Lillian's body trembled as the pricker approached. His cold, calculating gaze swept over her, devoid of any compassion or humanity. The air became colder, as if it foretold the pain and distress to come.

"Take off the dress. Don't want it impeding my tool." The pricker held up his torture device for her to see. The long, tapered needle imbedded in a wooden handle shined under the dim torchlight, its sharp tip reflecting the torment that awaited her.

Once Lillian had removed her dress and chemise, she stood shivering from the chill and embarrassment. Her face flushed, lips trembled.

"We are starting with that mark on your shoulder. The Inquisitor insisted I start there." The pricker drove in the needle.

Lillian screamed. Ean screeched from his perch on the window.

"He was right. It is not a witch's mark. The Devil hides them well so we will test all the usual places." The pricker grabbed her hand and plunged the needle into her palm near the base of her thumb.

Another scream burst forth as she tried to pull away but he tighten his grip, a sadistic smile on his face. "I guess that's not it."

Ean continued screeching and hopping on the windowsill. "I see you have your familiar close by. Where does he feed? I will find it."

The pricker continued his hunt. Lillian's body convulsed in agony, her cries stifled as her tormentor reveled in her suffering. Little streams of blood trickled down her flesh, a dreadful testament to their brutal quest for evidence.

"Do you want to confess and be done?"

Lillian shook her head. Through the haze of pain, she refused to surrender to their injustice. She clenched her teeth, determination burning within her, fueling her resilience. With every prick, she fought to keep her composure, the searing pain etching itself into her very being.

As the day wore on, her body bore the scars of their cruelty. Blood stained her skin, a reminder of the torture she had endured. But beneath the physical wounds, a fire blazed within her, a determination to expose the cruelty and inhumanity that plagued their society.

Lillian's mind was a mix of emotions—pain, anger, and a burgeoning sense of rebellion. She would not allow herself to be broken by their sadistic games. She would rise, stronger and more resilient than ever before, a testament to the indomitable spirit that lived within her.

In the depths of her suffering, Lillian made a silent vow. She would not rest until she brought justice to the Inquisitor and his cohorts.

And as the pricker continued his ruthless assault, Lillian locked eyes with him, her gaze defiant. She would endure, she would survive, and she would fight for a future where she could do as she damn well pleased.

CHAPTER TWENTY

LILLIAN STRODE, SHOULDERS BACK, chin up through the stifling chamber as the guards escorted her. She scanned the sea of faces that had congregated to witness her downfall. They had brought pews from the nearby church to oblige the ever-expanding crowd. The windows teemed with curious onlookers, their gazes fixated on her.

The Inquisitor and two Church members, projecting airs of authority, stood behind the magistrate. Had they pushed for this? In her own hometown, these enforcers of faith sought to control every aspect of life. Of course, their inescapable influence extended its overpowering grip to this place as well.

The magistrate's gavel rose and fell, a resounding thud against the podium. It shattered the din in the room, giving to a tense silence that hung in the air. "Lillian Maguire," he said, "you stand accused of witchcraft. Do you have anything to say in your defense?"

What words could she offer that would sway the biased minds that surrounded her? Bereft of representation and denied access to her cherished tarot cards, which had long guided her steps. "I beseech this court to recognize my innocence," Lillian said. "I am naught but a healer, a vessel of compassion."

Behind her, a discord of voices erupted, casting damning accusations into the air. "Witch!" they bellowed, their frenzied outcry threatening to drown out reason.

The magistrate's brow furrowed, and he wielded his gavel until the tumult subsided. "The court shall now hear the evidence against you," he said, his tone solemn. He sat in a chair in front of the bishop.

First to take to the podium was the sister of her neighbor, her grief-stricken countenance a mask for the fervor that burned within her. "My sister's labor was long and hard. We feared we were losing her. Her husband fetched this witch," she said, pointing at Lillian, "to help. I told him not to since she reads the cards, a sure blasphemy. But he was too afraid to lose his wife and the baby. The witch placed her head on my sister's belly. Then she pulled out black candles and lit them. She called for a spirit to assist her. Maybe it was the devil." She shook her head. "I don't know because I couldn't understand her words. Finally, the baby came, silent, not breathing. He had a long tail and tiny horns on the top of his forehead. Then I fainted. The next day, the cow gave sour milk, and the crops withered. My sister is not the same anymore." The woman put her hands to her face and sobbed. Even the magistrate's skeptical gaze betrayed a hint of intrigue at her testimony.

Lillian's jaw clenched, her knuckles turning white as she fought to keep her composure. The room seemed to darken, as if the weight of their accusations pressed upon her, threatening to snuff out her spirit.

Then came the testimony of the wheat farmer. His voice quivered and his eyes appeared distant and unfocused. "The hounds wouldn't stop barking. I had to go see what was going on. That's when I discovered her unclothed by my stream, dancing around, these tiny demons cavorting beside her. The Devil himself appeared in front of my eyes, reaching out to her. I feared for my life, but when I fired my rifle at her, she vanished into thin air and reappear in the Devil's arms, where they had an immoral act. The only reason I am standing here today is I recited Psalm 23:4 over and over when the Devil chased me. Later, a curse flatten my fields, revealing huge symbols of witchcraft. Now, I don't know what I'm going to do. She brought the Devil to my door." As he left the podium, his gaze focused on the Archbishop, who nodded.

A symphony of shock, fascination, and revulsion played out in the crowd, mixed with the thudding of Lillian's heart and her shallow, gasping breaths. The twisted account spun a web of condemnation, ensnaring her in the silvery silks of collective delusion.

The magistrate rose to speak at the podium. "Will the Inquisitor give his report?"

Not bothering to approach the podium, the Inquisitor said, his voice booming, "I used the prescribed method by prominent witch hunters to test Lillian Maguire. The first test was reciting the Lord's Prayer, which she was unable, a failing that proved indubitable evidence of witchcraft. I allowed her several attempts, but the Devil would not permit the words to be uttered." The magistrate rose, but the Bishop placed his hand on his shoulder to restrain any attempt to interject. His face dropped, and he sat back down, head bowed in submission.

The Inquisitor cast his eyes at the magistrate, eyes hooded. He lifted his head, closing his eyes before he addressed the crowd again. "I must remind you of the unholiness we witness when we trussed crosswise and placed Lillian Maguire into the River Shannon. The

Devil lifted her above the water, a sacred element of judgment, to show us his power. He demonstrated how he can defy the laws God has put upon us. It showed us her guilt." He lifted his index finger. "Yet, it compelled me to press further, to delve deeper into this enigma that is her existence. I continued my pursuit of the truth." When he lowered his hand, it disappeared into the folds of his cloak.

"Witches have marks the Devil leaves when he claims them for himself. There is speculation that he feeds from that mark." The Inquisitor paused while a collective murmur of agreement rippled through the crowd. He strode to Lillian. Each step carried an air of unapologetic confidence, as if he owned the ground beneath his feet. He reached out, his cloak whipping behind him, and pulled at her dress, baring her shoulder for all to see. "Behold, her mark." The room broke out into a frenzy. The sight of Lillian's birthmark fueled their conviction.

From within his cloak, The Inquisitor pulled out a paper and unfolded it. He stood, chin jutted, eyebrows raised, while a sneer spread across his face. "I have the report from the Witch Pricker I had summoned from Dublin."

Lillian never credited the Pricker as a literate man. She doubted he wrote anything. The walls of deceit had already reached the ceiling. They left no room for the truth.

"I performed my services as requested. She showed no reaction to a needle at the witch's mark or any usual place of a hidden mark. In addition, I must report that I feared for my life when the cell became so cold, my frigid fingers could barely hold my pricker. Every breath filled my soul with mortal dread in that icy chamber."

The Inquisitor bowed his head. "That concludes the testing."

The magistrate's gaze locked onto Lillian's own. "Having heard the evidence, this court finds Lillian Maguire guilty of witchcraft," he said, each word like a tolling bell heralding her doom. "You shall be burned at the stake."

A fiery rage erupted within Lillian, her nostrils flared as she leaned forward. She said, lip curled, "You condemn me based on tales spun from fear and ignorance. But mark my words, the truth will unveil its face, and your judgment shall crumble beneath the weight of its own injustice."

The room exploded into chaos, and the magistrate found himself powerless to regain control over the fervent mob.

The guards closed in around her. Lillian's hands balled into fists, muscles tightened in readiness to fight until the bitter end.

She refused to allow their twisted tales to define her, to extinguish the fire that burned within her. As they led her away, her head held high, she vowed to break free from the shadows of ignorance and superstition.

Deep within her heart, Lillian knew that true justice would prevail, even if she had to wage a relentless battle with every fiber of her being. As the heavy doors closed, she felt emboldened to take on the evil forces against her. *I will emerge like a butterfly, unbroken and triumphant.*

The guards brought Lillian out to the city square. The crowd pressed in around her, their hands clutching witch bottles filled with odd bits of items like nails, pins, herbs, and bones. She scoffed at their pitiful attempt to protect themselves from her powers. Her laughter echoed through the air like a defiant thunderclap. How foolish they were to believe that such trinkets could shield them from her wrath.

Her eyes flicked to the cruel Inquisitor, his heart as black as the depths of the abyss. A wicked smile curled upon her lips, for she knew that his position demanded such darkness.

The stake, a grotesque monument to their misguided beliefs, loomed before her. Logs piled high, a macabre pyre prepared for her burning. Clutching the sticks they had collected, the children scurried around with innocent joy, happy to play a role in the serious event.

As they brought Lillian to a platform built for the magistrate, the mayor, and the Church dignitaries, the weight of her impending fate hung heavy in the air. The magistrate asked, "Do you have any last words?"

Her laughter rang out again, a cascade of derision and defiance. She closed her eyes and spoke, bitterness and vengeance wrapped around every word. "I call out to Goddess Morrigan for retribution. I pray she send a pox on your potatoes and let you starve. The dying will bury the dead until you are no more. So mote it be!" She opened her eyes and stared at the Bishop in his most regal attire. "The Church will be helpless as it always has. False promises, that's all you have."

The Inquisitor nodded, a signal to the execution guards who approached Lillian, taking her from the prison guards. After they led her to the stake, one guard locked her arm shackles to an iron ring imbedded at the top of the stake, securing her in place. The other attached her leg shackles to the bottom ring. With each clank of metal, the chains of her captivity grew stronger. The guards re-treated, leaving her alone for the official lighting of the pyre.

Lillian pursed her lips and blew forth a powerful flame that danced at her feet. The wood below the stake caught fire, and soon the flames licked the sky. A collective scream erupted from the crowd as they recoiled, their faces twisted in terror.

Her laughter continued, growing louder and more manic. Wicked delight gleamed in her hooded eyes when she gazed upon the Inquisitor, the archbishop, the bishop, and the magistrate. They were all responsible for this cruel fate, and now they would witness the true power of her rare witchcraft.

She spotted the wheat farmer in near the platform, guilt etched on his face. He had lied about her, condemned her to this fate. Time for retribution. She directed a searing flame from her fire towards him using a mere flick of a finger, engulfing him in a vortex of fire. The crowd scattered in panic, leaving him screaming until he crumpled to the ground, consumed by the very flames that sought to devour her.

The church and town leaders shouted for the fire to be extin-guished, their panicked voices mingled in the chaos that surrounded them. But Lillian had no intentions of sparing them. She blew forth her breath within a sly smile, her fingers fanning out towards the Inquisitor. A droplet formed from her mouth, growing larger until it encased him, a watery prison from which he struggled to escape, gasping for breath.

She continued her relentless assault, directing more drops to snare the archbishop, the bishop, and the magistrate. They flailed, drown-ing in her liquid embrace. Her cackles filled the air as she watched them succumb in their watery graves. A simple poke of her finger burst the bubbles one by one, their lifeless bodies falling to the ground with resounding thuds.

Lillian reveled in her power, using earth, wind, fire, and water in various ways to strike fear into the hearts of every onlooker. Yet, amidst the chaos, there stood the old woman who had once spoken of the Irish Lady's Tresses by the wheat farmer's stream. She stood there, her gaze unwavering, unaffected by the havoc Lillian wrought. A slight smile played upon her weathered face, leaving Lillian uncertain of her true intentions. *Friend or foe?* The question had plagued her during her imprisonment. She did not testify in court against her, but she might have been the instigator by telling her the story of the orchids.

But it mattered not, for this was Lillian's fire, and she alone would decide when it would be extinguished. She hung there, suspended between life and death, her smugness palpable as she awaited when the stake burned to ash.

With a surge of determination, she began her liberation. Her shackled legs, bound to the stake, were now freed. She waited, occasionally tugging at the iron ring above her, testing its resistance. And when the moment proved favorable, she yanked herself to one side, avoiding the swing of the ring, for she desired no injury in her triumph.

Now liberated from the inferno that they had sought to consume her, Lillian stepped out of the fire unscathed. The flames leaped and danced, their tendrils reaching out in futile desperation, unable to touch her. The crowd gasped in disbelief, their eyes wide with awe and terror, witnessing a power that defied their understanding.

Her laughter echoed through the square once more, triumphant and satisfied. She cast a disdainful gaze upon the dead bodies of the church and town leaders who had orchestrated this spectacle of injustice.

The old woman remained unmoved, her eyes locked on Lillian, her bearing serene yet mysterious. "You possess a power greater than their comprehension," she said. "But take heed, for the path you choose will shape your destiny. Revenge and destruction will only perpetuate the cycle of darkness."

Lillian's gaze hardened, her determination resolute. "They will pay for what they have done to me, to others like me. The flames of my wrath will consume them all."

The old woman's eyes softened, a hint of sadness flickering within them. "True power lies not in vengeance, but in the choices we make. Seek justice, not retribution. Let compassion guide your actions, for in doing so, you may yet find redemption."

Lillian's expression wavered, the echoes of the old woman's words seeping into her consciousness. A flicker of doubt mingled with her burning rage. Could there be another way? A path that transcended the darkness that had consumed her?

As the embers of the stake smoldered behind her, Lillian stood at the crossroads of her destiny. The power she wielded, both fearsome and intoxicating, begged for direction. And in that moment, she realized her choices would shape not only her own fate but also the world that lay before her.

With newfound resolve, Lillian turned her back on the crowd, leaving them bewildered and trembling. As she ventured forth, her laughter carried on the wind.

Chapter Twenty-One

LILLIAN'S GAZE FIXED ON the dirt road, her steps cadenced, as she made her way towards her empty home. The weight of her shackles dragging along the ground served as a constant reminder of the oppression she had endured. The iron ring attached to her leg shackles grated against the rough surface, adding a haunting rhythm to her solitary march.

Lillian longed for the familiar voices and warm embraces that were nowhere to be found. Her family, once the pillars of her existence, had fled. Fear and misunderstanding had painted her as a monster. She became a threat to their very lives. The isolation she now faced bore was bitter, leaving her to navigate a treacherous path alone.

Ean, his feathers shimmering in the fading light, perched atop the shed. He observed the scene with his sharp mockingbird eyes, a silent witness to her plight.

Within the confines of the shed, Lillian rummaged through the tools, her fingers tracing their cold metal surfaces. Each object held the promise of freedom, a chance to sever the physical manifestation of her captivity. She gripped the hammer, pouring all her strength into a futile attempt to break the unyielding links. Frustration etched lines upon her face as her efforts fell short to shed the chains that bound her both physically and emotionally.

Undeterred, she called upon her elemental prowess, conjuring flames that danced with an ethereal light. With a steady stream of fire, she heated the metal, channeling her fury and determination into this delicate task. The pick found its mark, wedging itself within the weakened chain. She applied pressure, coaxing it to surrender to her will. The struggle continued, the sounds of strain mingling with the flickering of her inner fire.

At last, the chains shattered, granting her newfound freedom of movement. And time to notice a change.

Lillian's hair, touched by her own magick, had taken on an otherworldly hue. White strands cascaded around her face and across her shoulders, shimmering with an eerie, inner radiance.

In an act of defiance against societal norms and the oppressive dogma of the church, Lillian discarded the scarf that had concealed her true self. No longer would she cower in fear of persecution. The world would witness her strength, her power, and the fire that coursed through her veins.

With her resolve ignited, Lillian made her way inside her forsaken home, packing what possessions she could carry. She tended to the horse, her touch gentle and grateful for the loyal companion that stood by her side. With the horse in tow, she set out towards the distant cave, her heart filled with hope for a new beginning and a chance to start anew, alone.

Thoughts churned in her mind, forming plans and visions of a life untethered from the shadows of the past. She knew of a valley several days' journey away, where nature thrived in all its splendor. A sanctuary where she could find solace and unleash her green thumb upon the earth. Perhaps there, she could shed her name, forging a new identity in the embrace of a land untouched by the judgement of those who knew her.

But before her departure, one task remained—seeking answers from the enigmatic old woman who had guided her down a treacherous path. Doubt lingered, suspicions festered. Was the tale of the Irish Lady's Tresses an illusion designed to ensnare her? Was the old woman a rival witch, threatened by Lillian's arrival in town? The truth awaited her, and she vowed to uncover it before bidding farewell to this place forever.

Lillian took one last look back at the home she had with a husband and two daughters, now gone, all gone. A gust of wind whispered through the trees, carrying with it the echoes of her resolve. She turned away and looked at a new chapter of her life.

Lillian turned down the Main Road, her thoughts focused on the peculiar woman, the sound of her voice echoing in her mind. The Shannon River flowed alongside her, its waters reflecting the sunlight like shards of a shattered mirror. Where only days prior, they tried to drown her. The sight of a house with a magnificent garden caught her attention. The garden burst forth from its stone fence, vibrant colors cascading in a riotous display.

Certain that she had arrived at the right place, Lillian pushed open the gate and strode forward, her newfound white hair cascading over her shoulders. She reached the door and rapped her knuckles against the worn wood; the sound reverberating through the silence. In an instant, the door swung open, revealing the old woman standing before her.

"Who are you?" Lillian's voice held an edge, her eyes narrowing as she regarded the woman.

The woman gave a cryptic reply with a mischievous smile and a wink. "Just an old lady extending a hand of friendship to the new witch in town."

Lillian's glare deepened, her hands finding their way to her hips. "No. Who are you really? And why did you lead me to the Irish Lady's Tresses?"

The old woman's smile lingered, a knowing gleam in her eyes. "It matters not now. You are bound for a life in a cave, an odd choice of dwelling."

Then, as if fate itself willed it, Lillian's gaze shifted, catching sight of an orb weaver spider nestled in the corner of the door frame. Understanding dawned upon her—a realization that the woman's familiar had been in her company all along. The mysterious encounters on the road, the chance meetings in town—the pieces fell into place. Her suspicions confirmed. Trust was a rare commodity.

A mixture of anger and disappointment fueled Lillian as she turned on her heels, ready to leave. But first a measure of vengeance. Flames erupted from her fingertips, engulfing the once-thriving garden, reducing it to ash. She called for the crows, a cacophony of crows, their raucous calls echoing through the air, perched upon the witch's roof like a somber murder.

"Come, Ean," Lillian called to her mockingbird familiar. "Let us leave this little witch to her newfound companions. She has much work to do tending to her garden."

As Lillian ventured forth, a pang of concern for the people she left behind tugged at her heart. Rotting potatoes and the specter of new fevers would cast a grim shadow over the landscape. But she had solace in knowing that her children and brother had set sail for America—a land of opportunities. Though she would never lay eyes upon them again, breaking her promise to join them, she vowed to wield her magick, weaving spells of fortune from afar. Stella, with her indomitable spirit, would thrive regardless, but Mary, so akin to Lillian herself, remained a cause for concern.

Lillian was bound for a life in seclusion within the depths of a cave, hidden away from the world's prying eyes. Perhaps she would hunt for faeries, leprechauns, and banshees.

THE END

Sign up for my newsletter to get the scoop on future books in the series at https://www.annettegrantham.com/newsletter-signup/

The next book in the series answers the question of what happened to Stella and Mary.

I would greatly appreciate it if you left a review wherever you purchased this book.

Acknowledgements

A walk in the park or to the community pool in Brooklyn was an opportunity for my grandfather, Louis Clemente, to spin a tale, mostly spaghetti westerns. That's where my interest in storytelling began. As I grew, I filled notebooks with stories.

Then the push to become a doctor when I grew up took up more and more time. I didn't become a doctor, though. I finished college with a degree in Computer Science by way of a tour in the US Army.

Working and raising a family took up all my time, but I told my children stories. They especially remember the one where aliens used cardboard boxes of puppies to abduction humans.

In 2008, I discovered NaNoWriMo. Every November, I fit in time to write another novel. Some years I won, and some I didn't when I let life get in the way. But I have some bad novels stuffed away now. They say you have to write a million words before you write something good. NaNoWriMo helps you get those words written.

Through NaNoWriMo, I discovered the Lewis County Writers Guild. When Covid hit, we met by Zoom to critique each other's work. This is where I honed my skills. Amy F., Jim M., Margie K., Wayne W., Bev G., and Johanna F. are my tribe and I can't thank them enough.

Jim M. told me about the 20Booksto50K group on Facebook and that's where my writing and marketing education really began. I attended the conferences in Las Vegas and learned about story structure and newsletters. I received encouragement to publish and here I am.

Margie K. volunteered to read this novel and gave me feedback to fix some holes. There is nothing more valuable than a good beta reader. I am in her debt.

None of this would be possible without the love and support from my partner and soul mate, Dale Grantham. He understands my need to get up at 5:30am to write for a few hours. My dog, Twilight, deserves some credit in making sure I get some fresh air no matter the weather before I hit the keyboard.

Last but not least is you, the reader, for reading my novel all the way to the end. I thank you. I hope you enjoyed it and will leave a review somewhere. Your feedback is invaluable. More books are coming, I promise. I know you want to know what happened to Lillian's daughters, Stella and Mary. There's more to tell.

About the Author

Annette Grantham has always been a wanderer and an adventurer. Born in New York, she spent her childhood and youth moving across the Northeast coast and Texas. She joined the Army and served her country with pride. She then pursued a career as a software engineer. But her true passion was always writing.  She dreamed of crafting stories that would transport readers to magical worlds full of wonder and danger. Now she writes fantasy novels that combine her love of history and magic. Her five-book series, The Frontier Witches, is a thrilling blend of Deadwood and Practical Magic, featuring strong and sassy heroines who use their powers to survive and thrive in the lawless lands of the Old West. She lives with her high school sweetheart and her crazy dog in a cozy cabin surrounded by nature and a family of ravenous squirrels.

You can follow her by way of her newsletter (https://www.annetegrantham.com/newsletter-signup) or the following social medias:

Facebook: AnnetteGranthamAuthor

Instagram: dolphinladee

Threads: dolphinladee

Pinterest: annetteggrantham

Website: annettegrantham.com